哈福

2018新制多益 RC高分關鍵書

5 天 完 勝
突破極限，完美考高分
Reading Comprehension

讀霸
多益閱讀 模擬/測驗

[我的第一本閱讀入門書]

張瑪麗 · Steve King ◎合著 附MP3

哈福

我的第一本聽力閱讀入門書

任何一種語言，都是先從「聽」開始，就像嬰兒也是先「聽」了不少話，才開始學會「説」。所以廣泛的聽力訓練，對記憶單字、句型理解、文法組織……等學習的確獨具潛移默化的功效。要提高聽力，應選擇自己有興趣的，並且適合自己程度或稍高於自己程度的教材著手，真正紮實的練習是避免搭配文字資料來辨讀，純粹聽內容，不看書，反覆聽直到聽懂為止，這樣才能提高辨音理解能力。

「聽」與「説」是相輔相成的

本書所錄製之精質 MP3，是以一般外籍人士説話的正常速度來唸一遍，藉此提升讀者熟悉母語國家人士的語調和速度，並以此來檢視自己的聽力。最好能在經過幾天的聽力訓練之後，看看聽力程度有沒有進步，本來可能跟不上錄音速度，多聽幾遍反覆練習之後，相信你一定會有驚人的發現。

知識的累積需要閱讀，任何紮根與奠基的學習都必須藉由閱讀來累積辭藻及功力，多閱讀多吸收，英語能力自然而然就提昇。為了提供大小讀者補充英語閱讀材料的不足，本書精選幽默小短篇大約 50 則，各篇皆有精采的中文譯解，方便讀者參考對照，內容多元，囊括生活中各種情境的主題，有學校生活、期中末報告或考試、朋友之間、圖書館借書、娛樂、運動、休閒、情緒表達、分手、突發事件、各種場合應對……等等超級豐富的文章。

另外融合短文情境，衍伸書中人物幽默風趣的精采對話，尤其可運用於日常生活中，或是作為英語寫作範本。每篇搭配有 Q&A 小測驗，可加強測試您的聽力閱讀成果。不啻為全方位加強聽、說、讀、寫四大能力的基石，有效精進個人英文水平，迅速使您達到多元學習的目標。

本書由專業英語作家精心撰寫，帶您進入英語閱讀的美麗境界，突破傳統閱讀枯燥無味的學習法，符合時代流行新趨勢，兼具趣味及實用雙重特性，激發讀者想要自修上進的積極動力。本書適用於廣大英語愛好者，更是學生搶先儲備基本學力測驗、升學考試，或一般大眾英語能力檢定的最佳利器。

考試輕鬆入關，旅遊放膽出關

本系列書有幾大特色，能夠讓你臻至「考試輕鬆入關，旅遊放膽出關」的絕對效果，目前分別有「聽霸！英語聽力模擬測驗」、「讀霸！多益閱讀模擬測驗」，搭配學習，聽、說、讀、寫四大基本英語能力迅速加倍進化，不啻為你學習英語的神奇護照。

聽力和閱讀是學英文二個重要的關鍵，也是最難的關卡，一定要打通這任督二脈，尤其想要參加新制多益考試的人，更要加強這二項英文能力，當然每個人也都很想知道：要如何提升自己的聽力和閱讀能力？以便提高聽力測驗分數、閱讀測驗分數。

聽力測驗和閱讀測驗，二者比重一樣，所以任何一項都不能輕忽，本系列的第一本書是，談的是聽力測驗，針對全新多益 Part3 的簡短對話，進行教學和訓練；第二本書，談的是談閱讀測驗，針對全新多益 Part7 的單篇閱讀，進行教學和訓練。

進考場前，你已經先馳得點

如何強化聽力 & 閱讀能力？想要有好的學習效果，必須要針對新制多益的出題方向來考慮策略。首先要分析出在新制多益考試要具備多少的單字、文法能力，將出題可能性較高的重要單字、文法，集中起來學習才是良策；而且自己的單字、文法能力到底達到什麼程度，了解哪個領域，是自己比較弱的地方是很重要的。

新制多益考試有 13 個主要的出題方向：一般商務、

企業發展、辦公室、製造業、旅遊、外食、娛樂、保健、金融／預算、人事、採購、技術層面、房屋／公司地產。不論聽力或閱讀測驗，考題都是來自這 13 個情境。

　　考試的勝負往往決定於困難部份的分數，像聽力測驗中的簡短對話、簡短獨白部份，閱讀測驗的單句填空、和短文填空部份，是大家比較容易掌握的部份。若想脫穎而出拿高分，一次拿到金色證書，就要在別人不會的方面下功夫。但是話又說回來，二者相較，還是基本功比較重要，畢竟得分容易，基本分數先拿到再說，接下來再進攻比較艱深的考題，才不會兩頭落空，畢竟「手上一隻鳥，勝過林中二隻鳥」。

　　本書是想參加多益測驗者的第一本聽力閱讀入門書，前面說過閱讀測驗的單句填空、短文填空和單篇閱讀部份，是大家比較容易掌握、比較容易得分的部份，所以本書先著重在這個部份，以好拿分數者為優先學習，因為，有了基礎功，比較容易穩定軍心、建立自信心，讓你在上考場前，擁有比別人有更紮實的基礎和拿分的技巧，精讀本書後，進考場前，你已經先馳得點了。

CONTENTS

3. Sports & Exercise 球賽和運動

4. Trip 旅行

5. Express Feelings 表達感覺

6. Talking about Events 談論事件

7. Need Help 需要幫忙

1. At School

在學校

MP3-2

a. First day of school
第一天上學

Bobby was nervous about his first day at school. He had to get on the bus, and it was his first time to ride the bus. It wasn't so bad, he decided. When he entered his class, everyone seemed to be staring at him. Soon, though, he realized that they weren't staring at him but rather at every new student. He realized that everyone was equally nervous about their first day of school.

"Hey, I'm Joe," a fellow student sitting next to Bobby introduced himself.

"I'm Bobby," he replied. Bobby's first

day of school wasn't so bad. After all, he did make a new friend.

That day, he met many other people, too. However, none of them would become as good a friend as Joe.

中譯

巴比第一天上學時感到有些緊張。他得坐巴士去，而這也是他第一次坐巴士。應該不會太糟糕的，他心想。當他進入教室時，每個人似乎都盯著他看。不過，很快地，他知道他們並不是盯著他，而是幾乎盯著所有的新學生。這下他知道其實每個人都因為第一天上學而感到緊張呢！

「嗨，我是喬。」坐在巴比旁邊的同學向他自我介紹。

「我叫巴比，」他回答。巴比第一天上學沒有想像的那麼糟。他至少交了一個新朋友。那天，他還遇見了許多其他的人。不過，他們後來都不如喬和他的交情那麼好。

Question:

1. Who is Bobby's new friend?

    （誰是巴比的新朋友？）

    (A) Jake

    (B) Joe

    (C) Rachel

    (D) Aaron

    Answer: (B)

2. How did Bobby feel about his first day of school?

    （巴比對於第一天上學，感覺如何？）

    (A) Happy

    (B) Sad

    (C) Nervous

    (D) He didn't care

    Answer: (C)

Conversation:

Joe: Are you nervous about your first day here?
（你今天第一次來，你很緊張嗎？）

Bobby: Yeah, I am. Are you?
（是呀。你呢？）

Joe: You bet. Everyone here is a little bit nervous.
（當然是，這兒每個人都有點緊張。）

So there's no reason to be shy.
（所以沒有什麼不好意思的。）

Bobby: I suppose you're right.
（我想你說得對。）

▶ Life is ten percent what you make it and ninety percent how you take it.

----I.Berlin

生活有百分之十在於你如何塑造它，有百分之九十在於你如何對待它。

----I. 柏林

Question:

1. What did Bobby suppose Joe was right about?

（巴比認為喬說對了什麼？）

(A) That there's no reason to be shy.

(B) That Bobby was shy.

(C) That Joe was nervous.

(D) That Bobby was nervous.

Answer: (A)

2. Who was nervous?

（誰感到緊張？）

(A) Bobby

(B) Joe

(C) Everyone else

(D) All the above

Answer: (D)

b. Midterm, test, or pop quiz
期中考、小考或臨時測驗　　　　MP3-3

Rob and Greg came out of the classroom separately, one shortly after the other.　Greg waited in the hallway for Rob. When he saw Rob, he walked over to him.

"What did you think of the test?" asked Greg.

"That test was a killer!" Rob said.

"That's odd," said Greg. "I thought it was pretty easy."

"Easy? The professor didn't go over anything of that material in class."

"Yes, but if you had done the assignments, you would have been familiar with everything on the test," Greg replied without mercy.

"Yeah, yeah. I suppose you're right," Rob said.

"Of course I'm right. I thought the test was easy and I have a good grade in the class."

中譯

勞勃和葛瑞格一個稍前，一個稍後分別走出教室。葛瑞格在走廊等著勞勃。他看到勞勃時，朝他走了過去。

「你覺得這次小考如何？」葛瑞格問。

「這個小考真要命！」勞勃説。

「那倒奇怪了，」葛瑞格説。「我覺得這次挺簡單的。」

「簡單？教授在課堂上根本沒有教過那些題材。」

「沒錯，但如果你做了家庭作業，你對小考裡的考題應該很熟悉才對。」葛瑞格毫不留情地回答。

「是呀，是呀。我想你是對的，」勞勃説。

「我當然是對的。我覺得小考很簡單，而且這一科我的成績一定會很高。」

Question:

1. What did Greg think of the test?

（葛瑞格認為小考如何？）

(A) He thought it was hard.

(B) He thought it was fast.

(C) He thought it was easy.

(D) He thought it was difficult.

Answer: (C)

2. What could Rob have done to improve his grade on the test?

（勞勃應該做什麼來提高小考的成績？）

(A) Partied

(B) Studied

(C) Cheated

(D) Done his assignments

Answer: (D)

Conversation:

Greg: Did you find out what you made on the test?
（你知道你的小考成績如何嗎？）

Rob: Of course. Did you?
（當然。你呢？）

Greg: How did you do?
（你的成績如何？）

Rob: I did all right.
（還不錯。）

I passed with a 75. You?
（我拿了 75 分，及格了。你呢？）

Greg: I got a 92.
（我拿了 92 分。）

I told you that you should have done the assignments.
（我跟你說過，你早該好好做家庭作業。）

Questions:

1.   Who did better on the test?

（誰的小考成績比較好？）

(A) Greg

(B) Rob

Answer: (A)

2.   Greg asked if Rob found out...?

（葛瑞格問勞勃是否知道……？）

(A) If he made the team

(B) What he made on the test

(C) What his girlfriend thought of him

(D) If he passed the test

Answer: (B)

c. Paper or project
寫報告或進行科研項目

MP3-4

Randy was thinking about what he was going to research for his school project when Elizabeth called, interrupting him. Throughout their conversation, he was trying to think of what he was going to do, but he couldn't.

"What are you going to do?" asked Elizabeth.

Randy tried to blurt something out, thinking that whatever came to his mind he would do. However, nothing came to mind.

"I don't know," Randy surrendered. "Do you know what you're doing?"

"I was thinking of doing my paper on Christopher Columbus," Elizabeth answered.

"Christopher Columbus?" he asked.

"You know. The guy who discovered America?" she answered.

"Yeah, I know who Columbus is. He just doesn't seem to be that interesting. Anyways, I have to get back to work on my own paper."

中譯

藍第正在思考學校的論文該以什麼為主題，伊莉莎白剛好打電話來，把他的思路打斷了。他們在講電話時，他一直試著要思考他的研究應該做什麼，但卻想不出來。

「你打算做什麼？」伊莉莎白問他。

藍第想要把任何出現在他腦海的東西脫口而出說出來。但是他腦中一片空白。

「我不知道，」藍第放棄了。「那妳已經知道要做什麼了嗎？」

「我在考慮以克里斯多弗‧哥倫布為主題寫報告，」伊莉莎白回答。

「克里斯多弗‧哥倫布？」他問。

「你知道的，那個發現美洲大陸的人？」她回答。

「知道，我知道哥倫布是誰，但他的題材看來不怎麼有趣。不管怎樣，我得繼續我自己的報告了。」

Questions:

1. Whom is Elizabeth doing her report on?

   （伊莉莎白的報告主題是誰？）

   (A) Isabella of Spain

   (B) Queen Elizabeth

   (C) Napoleon

   (D) Christopher Columbus

   Answer: (D)

2. Whom is Randy doing his report on?

   （藍第的報告主題是誰？）

   (A) Bob Dylan

   (B) Henry VIII

   (C) He doesn't know

   (D) Pope Pius IX

   Answer: (C)

Conversation:

Elizabeth: So, Randy, who did you end up doing your report on?
（那麼，藍第，你的報告最後決定以誰為主題？）

Randy: Sir Francis Drake.
（法蘭西斯‧德雷克爵士。）

Elizabeth: Why did you choose him?
（你為什麼選擇他？）

Randy: Because he was a pretty cool pirate.
（因為他是很酷的海盜。）

He raided the Spanish ports in South America.
（他掠奪西班牙在南美洲的海港。）

Then he circled all the way around the globe and eventually led the British in defeating the Spanish Armada.
（他還航行環繞地球，最後帶領英國人打敗西班牙無敵艦隊。）

讀霸！多益閱讀模擬測驗

Question:

1. Who did Sir Francis Drake defeat?

（法蘭西斯·德雷克爵士打敗了誰？）

(A) The Ottoman Turks

(B) The Spanish Armada

(C) The Americans

(D) The British fleet

Answer: (B)

2. Why did Randy choose Sir Francis Drake?

（藍第為什麼選擇法蘭西斯·德雷克爵士？）

(A) Because he was a nice astronaut

(B) Because he was a sentimental poet

(C) Because he was a cool pirate

(D) Because he was a glorious conqueror

Answer: (C)

d. Go to the library
去圖書館

MP3-5

Amanda had finished her book the day before, so she decided to go to the library and check out a new book. She looked around at the different sections—history, literature, and science fiction—but she couldn't quite find the section that she was looking for. She walked over to a librarian.

"Excuse me," she said. "Do you know where to find the romance section?"

"Certainly, it's right over there," the librarian replied.

"Thanks," said Amanda. She walked over to the romance section and began to look through the books.

中譯

阿曼達昨天已經讀完她在看的書，所以她決定前往圖書館找本新書。她在不同的藏書區：歷史區、文學和

科幻小説區隨便看著，但她找不到她想要找的藏書區。於是她走到圖書館員那兒。

「打擾一下，」她説。「你知道浪漫小説區在哪兒嗎？」

「當然，就在那一邊，」圖書館員回答。

「謝謝，」阿曼達説。她走到浪漫小説區，開始在書堆中找她要的書。

Questions:

1. Which section was Amanda looking for?

   （阿曼達要找哪一個藏書區？）

   (A) History

   (B) Science Fiction

   (C) Romance

   (D) Fantasy

   Answer: (C)

2. Who did Amanda ask for help?

（阿曼達向誰尋求協助？）

(A) Her friend

(B) The librarian

(C) The custodian

(D) The professor

Answer: (B)

Conversation:

Amanda: Do you know where the romance section is?

（你知道浪漫小說區在哪兒嗎？）

Librarian: Yes. It's right over there.

（知道。就在那兒。）

Amanda: Ah, yes, there it is.

（啊，好，我看到了。）

One more thing...

（再請教你……）

Librarian: Yes?

（什麼事？）

Amanda: Do you know if you have the latest Danielle Steele book?

（你是否知道你們有沒有丹尼爾·史提爾最新的著作？）

Librarian: Yes, we do.

（有的，我們有。）

It's actually on display in the new books section.

（它就陳列在新書區。）

Questions:

1. Which author was Amanda looking for?

（阿曼達找哪位作家的作品？）

(A) Danielle Steele

(B) Louis L'Amour

(C) Lord Byron

(D) William Shakespeare

Answer: (A)

2. Where was the book that Amanda was looking for located?

（阿曼達要找的書放在什麼地方？）

(A) In the middle of the shelf

(B) In the new releases section

(C) At the front of the store

(D) In the romance section

Answer: (B)

e. Friends
朋友

MP3-6

Moving from town to town every few years can make it hard to make new friends. This was Louis' problem: his father was in the military, so his family was constantly moving. He got to see lots of different places and meet lots of different people, but it was hard for him to make true friends.

Louis was able to find one friend by the name of Drake. Drake's father was in the military too, and it was perhaps a pure twist of fate that Louis' and Drake's fathers were stationed at the same base at the same time for the same period. This common link was what brought the two together, and even after they moved they kept in touch. Eventually, after the two became old enough to live on their own, they got an apartment together in New York.

中譯

　　每隔幾年就得由一個城鎮搬到另一個城鎮，使得交朋友很困難。這正是路易斯的問題；因為他父親是軍人，因此他家經常隨著調動而搬家。他去過許多不同的地方，也遇見許多不同的人，但要交個好朋友，對他實在太難了。

　　路易斯後來交了一位名叫德雷克的朋友。德雷克的父親也在軍隊服役，也許真的是因為命運的安排，路易斯和德雷克兩人的父親在同一時期都派駐在同一個基地工作。這種相同的連結令兩人成了朋友，即使他們各自搬家後，他們仍然保持聯絡。後來，兩個人都能獨立生活後，還一起在紐約市合租了一間公寓。

Questions:

1. What did Louis's father do for a living?

（路易斯之父的職業是什麼？）

(A) He was an oilman

(B) He was a politician

(C) He was a software engineer

(D) He was in the military

Answer: (D)

2. Why was it hard for Louis to make true friends?

（為什麼路易斯要交朋友很困難？）

(A) He moved around a lot

(B) He was not a very likeable guy

(C) He was very unfriendly

(D) He was ugly

Answer: (A)

Conversation:

Louis: Long time no see.
（好久不見。）

Drake: No kidding.
（那可不是。）

Remember that one time a while back when we got in trouble at school?
（還記不記得我們還在學校時期惹了麻煩的事？）

Louis: For beating up that kid who kept making fun of you?
（因為打了那個老是戲弄你的小鬼？）

Yeah, I remember.
（是的，我記得。）

Drake: You really hit him hard.
（你可把他打慘了。）

Louis: My father was so mad.
（我父親氣炸了。）

He yelled at me for it.
（他為此事把我臭罵一頓。）

Drake: Mine, too.
（我父親也一樣。）

Louis: Ah, those were the days.
（啊，真是往事如煙。）

Questions:

1. What did Louis and Drake get in trouble for at school?

（路易斯和德雷克在學校時惹過什麼麻煩？）

(A) Not showing up to class

(B) Beating up a kid

(C) Not doing their homework

(D) Cheating on a test

Answer: (B)

2. What was Louis's father's reaction?

（路易斯的父親有什麼反應？）

(A) He praised Louis

(B) He was ashamed

(C) He got drunk

(D) He yelled at Louis

Answer: (D)

33

2. Entertainment

娛樂

a. Movie
電影

MP3-7

Bob and his friends had decided to go see a movie. After a short discussion, they decided to go watch a comedy. Bob picked up the paper to see the movie listings and read them off so that his friends could hear. His friends listened half-attentively.

"There's 'Something About Mary', 'The Day after Tomorrow', 'Ghostbusters', and 'Snatch'," he read.

Kenny spoke up upon hearing the word "Snatch". "I heard Snatch is a great movie. Let's watch that one," Kenny said.

"I had a friend who saw it," Billy said.

"He said it was pretty good."

"That was me," Jonesy said. "It was a pretty good movie. I'd be willing to see it again."

Everyone agreed to go and watch "Snatch".

2

Entertainment 娛樂

中譯

鮑布和他的朋友決定去看場電影。經過短暫的討論，他們決定去看場喜劇。鮑布拿起報紙查看電影放映名單，並一邊唸著讓他的朋友也聽見。他的朋友不怎麼聚精會神地聽著。

「哈拉瑪莉」、「明天過後」、「魔鬼剋星」和「偷拐搶騙」，他讀著。

肯尼聽到「偷拐搶騙」時説話了。「我聽説『偷拐搶騙』是一部很棒的電影。我們看這部吧！」肯尼説。

「我有個朋友看過了。」比利説。「他説這部電影挺不錯的。」

「是我跟你説的。」瓊西説。「那的確是部好電影，我很願意再看一遍。」

大伙兒都同意去看「偷拐搶騙」。

Questions:

1. Who suggested that they go see "Snatch"?

（誰建議他們一起去看「偷拐搶騙」？）

(A) Bob

(B) Kenny

(C) Billy

(D) Jonesy

Answer: (B)

2. Where did Bob find the times and places for the movie?

（鮑布在哪兒找到電影的時間表和放映地點？）

(A) He called up the movie theaters.

(B) He checked the movie listings in the newspaper

(C) He looked them up on the internet

(D) He asked Billy

Answer: (B)

Conversation:

Bob: So what's 'Snatch' about, anyway?
（「偷拐搶騙」到底是部什麼樣的電影？）

Jonesy: It's about a bunch of jewel thieves.
（它是關於一群珠寶竊賊的電影。）

They all pretty much end up working for each other and they're all trying to steal the same jewel.
（他們最後都很願意彼此合作，竊取同一顆珠寶。）

Bob: Is it funny?
（這電影有趣嗎？）

Jonesy: It's hilarious.
（這電影很好笑。）

Questions:

1. What kind of thieves are in the movie?

（電影裡的小偷是什麼樣的小偷？）

(A) Cat burglars

(B) Muggers

(C) Jewel thieves

(D) Smugglers

Answer: (C)

2. How funny does Jonesy think the movie is?

（瓊西認為這部電影多有趣？）

(A) Not funny

(B) A little funny

(C) Really funny

Answer: (C)

b. TV
電視

MP3-8

Margaret hated when her husband, Joe, just sat on the couch and channel-surfed all evening long. When she complained, though, he would always say, "There's never anything good on TV. By the way, could you get me a beer?"

Of course, she would never get him his beer, and she also disagreed about never having anything good to watch on TV. They had a digital cable line installed three months ago and it brought them 568 channels of pure channel-surfing excitement.

Finally, Margaret had the sense to rip the controller from Joe's hand and flip to the preview guide screen. She was able to quickly locate which channel "Friends" was on and turned the TV on to "Friends."

中譯

　　瑪格麗特最討厭她丈夫喬整晚坐在沙發上，不斷地轉台看電視。但她報怨時，她丈夫總是説，「電視上從來沒有好節目。對了，能不能拿瓶啤酒給我？」

　　當然，她從來才不拿啤酒給他，她也不同意他認為電視上從來沒有好節目的説法。他們家在三個月前安裝了數位有線電視，總共有 568 個頻道可以讓他們轉個痛快。

　　最後，瑪格麗特懂得了由喬的手中奪下遙控器，並轉到節目介紹的頻道。她可以很快地找到「六人行」在哪個頻道播出，而把電視轉到「六人行」的頻道。

Questions:

1. What kind of television did Joe and Margaret subscribe to?

   （喬和瑪格麗特所訂的是哪一種電視轉播？）

   (A) Satellite TV

   (B) Digital cable

   (C) Basic cable

   (D) Antenna

   Answer: (B)

2. Where would Joe sit?

（喬坐在哪裡？）

(A) On the floor

(B) In a chair

(C) On the couch

(D) In a recliner

Answer: (C)

Conversation:

Margaret: Why do you always channel-surf?
（你怎麼老是在轉頻道？）

Joe: Because there's never anything good on TV.
（因為電視上從來沒有好節目。）

Margaret: There are tons of good things on TV!
（電視上的好節目可多了！）

That's why we subscribed to digital cable, isn't it?

（那不就是我們改訂數位有線電視的原因嗎？）

Joe: Okay. Name one good show that's on.

（好。那妳隨便說出一個正在播出的好節目。）

Margaret: Why don't you just flip it to the preview guide channel and see for yourself?

（你為什麼不轉到節目介紹頻道，自己看一看？）

Questions:

1. What did Margaret accuse Joe of doing?

（有關瑪格麗特指責喬的是什麼？）

(A) Channel-surfing

(B) Being a couch potato

(C) Getting fat

(D) Never doing anything

Answer: (A)

2. Which channel did Margaret tell Joe to flip it to?

（瑪格麗特要喬轉到哪個頻道？）

(A) A sports channel

(B) The preview guide channel

(C) A comedy channel

(D) The news station

Answer: (B)

c. Reading

閱讀　　　　　　　　　　　　　MP3-9

Julia had always thought of reading as a very relaxing way to end a busy day. Whenever she would come home from work, she would open up book and read it for about an hour. This she would do almost immediately and would never let anyone interrupt her special form of meditation. Even

if the phone rang or there was a knock on the door, she would ignore everything and completely immerse herself in her book.

She always taught her children that reading was the root of intelligence. That a well-read person was an educated person and one who was educated was better prepared to make decisions. She didn't care what kind of books her children read, just merely that they read, so that they could exercise their minds.

中譯

　　茉莉亞向來認為閱讀是忙碌的一天之後最後的精神調劑。她只要下班回到家裡，她總是會打開書本，大約讀上一個小時。她幾乎一回到家就馬上開始閱讀，而且絕不會讓人打擾到她有如冥思般的特別做法。即使電話響了或有人敲門，她都不予理會，並聚精會神地沈浸在她的書本中。

　　她一向教導她的孩子，閱讀是智慧的根源。一位經常閱讀的人是一位教育良好的人，而受到良好教育的人則擅於做決定。她不管她的孩子讀什麼書，因為只要他們閱讀，他們就能鍛鍊自己的智力。

Questions:

1. Julia taught her children that reading was the root of all _____.

   (茱莉亞教導孩子,閱讀是___的根源。)

   (A) Evil
   (B) Good
   (C) Intelligence
   (D) Stupidity

   Answer: (C)

2. Julia would read when she came home from what?

   (茱莉亞在做什麼之後回家即展開閱讀?)

   (A) Work
   (B) Jogging
   (C) Dating
   (D) School

   Answer: (A)

Conversation:

Julia: I can't wait to get home so I can finish my book.
（我巴不得趕快回家，我就可以讀完我那本書。）

Don: What book are you reading?
（妳讀哪本書？）

Julia: To Kill a Mockingbird.
（梅崗城故事。）

Don: That's a good book.
（那是本好書。）

I had to read that back in high school.
（我在高中時是必讀。）

Julia: It's the first time I've read it.
（這是我第一次讀這本書。）

Don: What do you think of it?
（妳認為這本書如何？）

Julia: I love it.
（我非常喜歡。）

Well, here's my stop. Goodbye.
（啊，我該下車了，再見。）

Questions:

1. What did Don think of To Kill a Mockingbird?

   (唐認為「梅崗城故事」如何？)

   (A) That it wasn't very well written.

   (B) That it was boring.

   (C) He didn't like it.

   (D) That it's a good book.

   Answer: (D)

2. When did Don read To Kill a Mockingbird?

   (唐在什麼時候讀了「梅崗城故事」？)

   (A) In grade school.

   (B) In high school.

   (C) In college.

   (D) He just finished it.

   Answer: (B)

d. Music
音樂

MP3-10

Jessica loved music, especially rock music. Everyday, as she drove to work, she would listen to whatever CD she had loaded in the player. She knew that the people sitting in the cars beside her could hear her music, but she didn't care. It was her way to cope with the world, simply to play the music as loud as she could handle as she drove.

On the weekends she would go to music concerts and dance her heart out to the beat of the drums. Sometimes people didn't understand her enthusiasm; sometimes people did. When she was near someone who didn't share her love for music, she would simply move until she was near someone that did.

中譯

潔西卡非常喜愛音樂，特別是搖滾樂。每天她開車

去上班時，她就隨手把音樂光碟放進光碟播放器中，看她放進什麼音樂，她就聽什麼音樂。她知道路上並行的駕駛人聽得到她的音樂，但她可毫不在乎。在開車時，把音樂開大到她自己所能忍受的音量，就是她應付外在世界的方式。

週末時，她去參加音樂會，並隨著鼓聲痛快地跳舞。有時候，人們並不了解她這種熱情，但也有人可以。如果她遇到不能和她共享她對於音樂的熱愛時，她就繼續向前，直到找到同樣喜愛音樂的人。

Questions:

1. To cope with the world, where would Jessica play her music loudly?

   （為了應付外在世界，潔西卡在哪裡把音樂開得很大聲？）

   (A) In her house

   (B) In her car

   (C) At her desk at work

   (D) In her backyard

   Answer: (B)

2. Through what medium did Jessica listen to her music in the car?

（潔西卡在車上使用什麼器材聆聽音樂？）

(A) Radio

(B) Tapes

(C) CDs

(D) None of the above

Answer: (C)

Conversation:

Jessica: Hey, Matt!
（嘿，馬特！）

Matt: I see you've got headphones on…
（你戴了耳機……）

Jessica: Yeah, I'm just enjoying my music.
（是啊，我正在聽音樂。）

Matt: What band are you listening to?
（你聽哪個樂團的音樂？）

Jessica: Gary Jules.
（蓋瑞・朱爾斯。）

Matt: Never heard of him.
（沒聽說過這個人。）

What kind of music does he do?
（他的音樂風格是什麼？）

Jessica: Rock.
（搖滾樂。）

2

Entertainment 娛樂

Questions:

1. Which band was Jessica listening to?

   （潔西卡聽什麼樂團的音樂？）

   (A) Pearl Jam

   (B) PPK

   (C) Nine Inch Nails

   (D) Gary Jules

   Answer: (D)

2. What kind of music does he do?

   （他的音樂是哪一種？）

   (A) Rap

   (B) Rock

   (C) Techno

   (D) Pop

   Answer: (B)

3. Sports & Exercise
球賽和運動

a. Football
足球

Aaron loved football and dreamed of one day playing in the Superbowl. In his backyard, he imagined himself running into the end-zone and scoring a touchdown, while thousands of fans were packed in the stands chanting his name: "Aaron! Aaron! Aaron!"

It was because of this dream that Aaron found himself standing in line for the football team tryouts during his first year of high school. Thus, a more realistic dream was that of leading his high school football team, the Panthers, to a state

championship victory every year that he was there. When his name was called, he smiled, thinking about the greatness he had before him.

中譯

　　亞隆非常喜愛足球，而且還夢想有一天能參加超級足球盃比賽。在他家的後院裡，他幻想自己衝入達陣區觸地得分，而無數的球迷則擠滿了觀球台，喊叫著他的名字：「亞隆！亞隆！亞隆！」

　　因為這個夢想，亞隆在高中一年級時，就去排隊參加選拔。也因此，一個比較實際的夢想就是在他就讀此校期間，帶領他的校隊，粉紅豹隊，每年得到州際比賽冠軍。他的名字被點到時，他微笑著想著即將來到的榮耀。

Questions:

1. What was Aaron's high school football team named?

   （亞隆的高中足球校隊叫什麼名字？）

   (A) The Panthers

   (B) The Pythons

   (C) The Buccaneers

   (D) The Trojans

   Answer: (A)

2. Where does one score a "touchdown"?

   （在哪兒可以「觸地得分」？）

   (A) At the home plate

   (B) At the end-zone

   (C) Mid-field

   (D) In the goal box

   Answer: (B)

3 Sports & Exercise 球賽和運動

Conversation:

Gina: Why do you like football so much?
（你為什麼這麼熱愛足球？）

Aaron: How can you not like it?
（怎能不喜歡？）

There's nothing more American than football, is there?
（再也沒有什麼比足球更美式，不是嗎？）

It's such a great sport.
（這是個超棒的運動。）

Gina: I just don't understand why it's a great sport.
（但我就是不懂這怎麼會是超棒的運動。）

And as for being American, baseball is more American, isn't it?
（而且，說到美式，棒球不是更美式嗎？）

Aaron: They're about the same, but football is better.
（它們都差不多，但足球更棒。）

Football has strategy.
（足球牽涉到策略的運用。）

It's like war.
（它就像戰爭一樣。）

Gina: And that's great?
（那樣算很棒嗎？）

Aaron: It's the American way!
（這就是美式風格！）

Questions:

1. Why does Aaron think football is better than baseball?

   （為什麼亞隆認為足球比棒球還棒？）

   (A) It's more exciting
   (B) More happens
   (C) It has strategy
   (D) The games are shorter

   Answer: (C)

2. What does Aaron say football is like?

   （亞隆認為足球像什麼？）

   (A) Baseball
   (B) War
   (C) Wrestling
   (D) Cooking

   Answer: (B)

3 Sports & Exercise 球賽和運動

b. Baseball

棒球

MP3-12

Baseball was the only way Melissa found that she could bond with her father. Because of that, she loved the sport. Her father was very distant with her as a child and was often more interested in watching sports on TV. However, when Melissa began taking an active interest in baseball, her father began taking an active interest in her.

Melissa's favorite childhood memories were of going to the baseball games with her father. They never got tired of watching their favorite team, the Cincinnati Reds. As a batter hit a homerun and rounded all the bases, Melissa and her father would stand up and scream their lungs out until he reached the home plate.

中譯

棒球是梅莉莎認為她唯一可以和她父親有所聯繫的

方式。因為這樣,她熱愛這項運動。在她小時候,她的父親和她很疏遠,而且他更熱衷於看電視運動節目。不過,當梅莉莎開始對棒球有熱切的興趣時,她的父親也同樣對她有更積極的關注。

梅莉莎最鍾愛的兒時記憶是和父親去觀看棒球賽。他們對於觀看他們最愛的球隊,辛辛那提紅人隊,熱情從不稍減。打擊手擊出全壘打並開始跑過全部的壘包時,梅莉莎和她父親總是會站起來,竭力吶喊,直到打擊手奔回本壘。

Questions:

1. **What was Melissa's favorite team?**

   (梅莉莎最喜愛的是哪一隊?)

   (A) The Baltimore Orioles

   (B) The Cincinnati Reds

   (C) The Boston Red sox

   (D) The New York Yankees

   Answer: (B)

3 Sports & Exercise 球賽和運動

2. What does a baseball player hit to allow them to "round all the bases"?

（什麼情況下，棒球選手可以「跑過各壘」？）

(A) A homerun

(B) A grounder

(C) A field goal

(D) A punt

Answer: (A)

Conversation:

Melissa: Thanks for taking me to the game, Dad!

（爸，謝謝你帶我去看球賽！）

Father: Anything for my daughter.

（只要我女兒喜歡的都好。）

Melissa: I think I'm going to go get some hot dogs.

（我想去買點熱狗。）

You want one?

（你要不要來一個？）

Father: Yeah. Actually, could you get me three?

（好呀。事實上，妳可以幫我買三個嗎？）

Here's some money.

（錢在這裡。）

Be sure to bring back the change.

（別忘了找錢回來。）

Melissa: Nah, I think I'll keep it as a tip.

（不，我要自己留下來當小費。）

Questions:

1. What is Melissa going to get?

（梅莉莎要去買什麼？）

(A) Hot dogs

(B) Beer

(C) Pizza

(D) Peanuts

Answer: (A)

3 Sports & Exercise 球賽和運動

2. How many does her father want?

（她父親要幾個熱狗？）

(A) One

(B) Two

(C) Three

(D) Four

Answer: (C)

c. Jogging
慢跑
MP3-13

"You've got to do something to stay in shape," my mother always told me. So when Angela asked me to go jogging with her, I decided that I might as well. After all, I had to do something to stay in shape, right?

I didn't realize it at the time, but she

wanted to jog at daybreak.

"You've got to get out there before it gets hot!" she told me upon seeing my reluctance to wake up so early. At first I hated jogging; every day, I would go home sore and tired. Eventually, though, I started liking it. Jogging became the rhythm of my life.

中譯

　　「妳得想想辦法維持身材，」我媽老是這麼告訴我。所以，當安琪拉問我要不要和她去慢跑時，我決定還是和她去好了。畢竟，我真的得做點什麼好維持身材，對吧？

　　不過我當時並不知道，她要在黎明時慢跑。

　　「妳得在氣溫變熱之前出去慢跑！」她看我對早起顯得厭煩時這麼說。一開始，我真討厭慢跑，我每天回家都感到酸痛和疲累。不過，慢慢地，我開始喜歡慢跑，慢跑現在已經融入我生活中的一部份了。

Questions:

1. When do Angela and I go jogging?

（安琪拉和我什麼時間去慢跑？）

(A) At dusk

(B) At daybreak

(C) After work

(D) At night

Answer: (B)

2. Why did I decide to start jogging?

（我為什麼決定開始慢跑？）

(A) To stay in shape

(B) I had nothing better to do

(C) Angela told me to

(D) I needed to lose weight

Answer: (A)

Conversation:

Angela: I told you that you would like jogging.
（我跟妳説過妳會愛上慢跑的。）

Me: Yeah, I was kind of surprised.
（對呀。我也感到有點驚訝。）

I didn't think I'd actually like it.
（我當時並不認為我會真的喜歡它。）

Angela: What do you mean?
（怎麼説？）

Me: Well, the only reason I started was because of you, but I actually started to like jogging.
（哎，我開始慢跑唯一的原因是因為妳，但我真的開始喜歡慢跑了。）

I'm feeling really good about myself.
（我覺得自己真的很棒。）

Angela: Exercise will have that effect on you.
（運動的確會帶給妳那樣的效果。）

Me: What? Feeling good?
（什麼？感覺很棒？）

Angela: That's right.
（一點兒沒錯。）

3 Sports & Exercise 球賽和運動

Questions:

1. How will exercise make you feel?

   （運動會讓你感到如何？）

   (A) Bad

   (B) Tired

   (C) Energetic

   (D) Good about yourself

   Answer: (D)

2. What was the only reason I started jogging?

   （我為什麼開始慢跑？）

   (A) Angela

   (B) Mother

   (C) Because it was healthy

   (D) Because I knew it would make me feel good

   Answer: (A)

d. Weights
舉重

MP3-14

Andrew placed the weights on his bench press. He stretched his arms, hoping to loosen up his muscles.

"Hey," he called to another person working out. "Can you help me out?"

"Sure," the man replied. The man came over and watched Andrew lift the weights, making sure that Andrew always managed to lift the weights himself.

"Looks heavy," the man said.

"It is," Andrew said in a strained voice. After Andrew set the weights down, he stretched his arms some more.

"How many more sets do you have left?"

"Well, I've already done three. That just leaves one more."

3

Sports & Exercise 球賽和運動

中譯

安德魯將舉重器放在舉重練習凳上。他伸展雙臂，想要放鬆肌肉。

「嘿，」他叫另一個正在健身的人。「你能幫我個忙嗎？」

「當然，」那個男人回答。他走了過來，看著安德魯舉起舉重器，確定安德魯能自行將舉重器舉起來。

「看來挺重的，」那男人說。

「是的，」安德魯勉力地說道。安德魯把舉重器放下後，他又伸展了幾次雙臂。

「你還有幾套要做？」

「我已經做了三套。現在只剩一套。」

Questions:

1. What kind of weights was Andrew doing?

（安德魯進行哪一種舉重？）

(A) Curls

(B) Squats

(C) Lunges

(D) Benches

Answer: (D)

2. How many sets did Andrew have left?

（安德魯還有幾套運動要做？）

(A) One

(B) Two

(C) Three

(D) Four

Answer: (A)

3

Sports & Exercise 球賽和運動

Dialogue:

Andrew: I can bench 210 pounds.
（我可以在練習凳上舉起 210 磅。）

What about you?
（你呢？）

Kyle: That's nothing.
（那不算什麼。）

I can bench 230 pounds.
（我在練習凳上可以舉起 230 磅。）

Andrew: Yeah? Well, I squat 675 pounds.
（是嗎？哪，我可以蹲著舉起 675 磅。）

Kyle: Well, I squat 750 pounds.
（啊，我蹲著舉起 750 磅。）

Andrew: I don't believe you.
（我才不相信。）

You're just going to say a weight greater than my own every time.
（你不過是每次都要說一個比我多的重量而已。）

Kyle: That's true, but that doesn't mean I'm lying.
（那倒是真的，但那可不表示我說謊。）

Questions:

1. How much weight can Kyle bench?

   （凱爾可以在練習凳舉起多少重量？）

   (A) 150 pounds

   (B) 210 pounds

   (C) 230 pounds

   (D) 280 pounds

   Answer: (C)

2. What kind of exercise do they compare the second time?

   （他們第二次比較什麼樣的運動？）

   (A) Squats

   (B) Bench

   (C) Lounges

   (D) Hurtles

   Answer: (A)

3 Sports & Exercise 球賽和運動

4. Trip

旅行

a. Planning
制定計劃

MP3-15

Walter loved going on trips, but he hated planning for them. He knew that it was important to plan out an itinerary, but his family would always complain about the tight schedule he would plan out.

Even their destinations were very carefully planned. He had his "Travel Book," in which he wrote down over a hundred locations that he would like to see. His wife once told him to just sit down and relax.

"Just throw a dart at a map, and that's where we'll go," she would say. "Then,

just get a hotel, and we'll head on over."

中譯

　　華特熱愛旅行，但是不喜歡作旅行規劃。他知道先規劃好行程很重要，但他的家人總是抱怨他定的行程太緊了。

　　他們的目的地甚至都經過妥善計畫。他在他的「旅行指引」書中寫下了超過一百個他想要去的地點。他的太太有次要他坐下來放輕鬆一點。

　　「在地圖上擲飛鏢，射中哪裡我們就去哪裡，」她說。「然後訂好旅館，我們就可以出發到那兒去了。」

Questions:

1. Walter had a tendency to _____ his vacations.

（華特對於度假有 _____ 的傾向。）

(A) under-plan

(B) over-plan

(C) miss

(D) hate

Answer: (B)

2. Where did Walter write down his travel destinations?

（華特將他的旅行目的地寫在何處？）

(A) In his "Travel Book"

(B) In his journal

(C) In his "Vacation Book"

(D) In the back page of the October 1999 issue of "National Geographic"

Answer: (A)

Dialogue:

Walter: This time we're going to Wyoming.
（這一次我們要去懷俄明州。）

Wife: Wyoming? Why Wyoming?
（懷俄明州？為什麼是懷俄明州？）

The kids and I want to go skiing in Colorado.
（孩子們和我都想去科羅拉多州滑雪。）

Walter: But we haven't been to Wyoming.
（但我們從沒去過懷俄明州。）

And you can ski there, too.
（而且你們在那兒也可以滑雪。）

Wife: But we want to go to Colorado.
（但是我們要去科羅拉多州。）

Why can't we go somewhere that we want to go?
（為什麼我們不能去我們想去的地方？）

Walter: But I want to go to Wyoming.
（但我要去懷俄明州。）

Don't you want to see Old Faithful?
（妳不想去看老忠實噴泉嗎？）

Wife: I want to go skiing in Colorado.
（我要去科羅拉多州滑雪。）

Questions:

1. **What does Walter's wife want to do?**

   （華特的妻小想去什麼地方？）

   (A) See Old Faithful in Wyoming

   (B) Hike in the Grand Canyon

   (C) Bungee jump off the Brooklyn Bridge

   (D) Ski in Colorado

   Answer: (D)

2. **What does Walter want to see in Wyoming?**

   （華特想去懷俄明州看什麼？）

   (A) Sequoia National Park

   (B) The London Bridge

   (C) Old Faithful

   (D) Tacoma Narrows

   Answer: (C)

b. The trip
旅行

MP3-16

Though Walter loved visiting places, he hated driving there. The kids would always be fighting in the back seat of the car, and his wife would tell him to pull over so she could use the restroom every five minutes. When they finally made it to their resort in Colorado, he gave a sigh of relief. The kids jumped out and started to play in the snow, and his wife took a huge breath of fresh air before running off to the restroom again. He laughed and stretched his back.

They skied for three days straight. He was so sore by the end of it that he was extremely reluctant to get in the car. He wasn't upset that his vacation was over; rather, he was not looking forward to the long drive home.

中譯

　　雖然華特喜歡去旅行,但他痛恨開車去目的地。孩

子們老是在車後座吵架，而他太太幾乎每隔五分鐘就要他靠邊停車，好讓她上廁所。終於，他們到了科羅拉多州的度假地，他也鬆了一口氣。孩子們快速地下了車，在雪地上玩耍，他的太太趕著去廁所之前也好好呼吸了一口新鮮空氣。他大笑著伸展他的背部。

他們在那兒整整滑雪滑了三天。最後，他全身酸痛，非常不情願地上了車。他並非為了假期結束而難過，他卻是一點兒也不想開這麼遠的路途回家。

Questions:

1. Where did Walter and his family go for their vacation?

（華特和家人到何處度假？）

(A) Las Vegas

(B) Colorado

(C) Wyoming

(D) San Francisco

Answer: (B)

2. What did his wife have to do a lot while driving to their destination?

（他太太在開車前往目的地途中，老是做很多什麼事？）

(A) Go to the restroom

(B) Eat

(C) Yell at the kids

(D) Complain

Answer: (A)

Dialogue:

Walter: Are you happy now that we're almost to Colorado?

（我們快要到科羅拉多州了，這下妳可樂了吧？）

Wife: Yes, I am. Very happy.

（是的，我很快樂。非常快樂。）

But I need to go to the restroom.

（但我得上廁所。）

Walter: Again? Didn't we just stop five minutes ago?

（又要上廁所？五分鐘之前我們不是才停下來過嗎？）

Wife: Yes, but I had something to drink.

（對呀，但我又喝了東西。）

Now, will you just pull over?

（現在，可不可以你請你停車？）

Walter: All right, all right.

（好吧，好吧。）

Questions:

1. How did Walter's wife feel about going to Colorado?

（華特的妻子對於去科羅拉多感覺如何？）

(A) Sad

(B) Dismayed

(C) Queasy

(D) Happy

Answer: (D)

2. **How long ago did they stop last?**

（他們上次停車是多久以前？）

(A) 5 minutes

(B) 10 minutes

(C) 15 minutes

(D) 20 minutes

Answer: (A)

c. After the trip
旅行之後

MP3-17

Walter and his family finally returned home. They had to unpack all of their things and throw their clothes into the washing machine. Walter's wife frowned because she knew that she would be the one to wash all of their dirty clothes.

"Did you kids have a fun time?"

Walter asked his boys.

"We sure did," they answered.

They were all sitting at the table, drinking hot cocoa, thinking about the trip. Walter suddenly remembered that he had things to do around the house, so he left to get things ready for work the next day.

中譯

　　華特和家人終於回到家。他們得把所有的行李打開，並把衣服丟入洗衣機。華特的妻子皺著眉，因為她知道她是得洗清這堆髒衣服的人。

　　「你們這幾個小鬼頭玩得愉快嗎？」華特問他的兒子們。

　　「我們玩得很高興，」他們回答。

　　他們全都圍著餐桌而坐，一邊喝著熱可可，一面回想著這趟旅行。華特突然想起家裡還有些事沒做完，於是起身準備明天的工作。

Questions:

1. Who was going to wash the clothes?

   （誰得洗衣服？）

   (A) Walter

   (B) The kids

   (C) Walter's wife

   (D) They were going to wash themselves

   Answer: (C)

2. What was the family drinking?

   （他們一家人喝什麼？）

   (A) Chocolate milk

   (B) Hot cocoa

   (C) Soda

   (D) Coffee

   Answer: (B)

Conversation:

Walter's wife: So did you end up enjoying yourself even though we didn't go to Wyoming?

（即使我們沒去懷俄明州，你終究是否玩得開心？）

Walter: Yeah, I suppose I did.

（有吧，我想是的。）

Wife: See? Things we want to do are fun, too.

（瞧見沒？我們想要做的也是很好玩的。）

Maybe you should listen to us more often.

（也許你應該多聽聽我們的意見。）

Walter: Actually, I don't really like that idea.

（事實上，我並不太喜歡那個主意。）

Wife: So then where are we going to go next time?

（那我們下回去哪裡呢？）

Walter: Wyoming, of course.

（懷俄明州，當然了。）

Questions:

1. What does Walter think of his wife's suggestion to listen to her more often?

   （華特對於他太太認為應該多聽她的建議反應如何？）

   (A) He doesn't like it

   (B) He agrees

   (C) He loves the idea

   (D) He thinks it sounds interesting

   Answer: (A)

2. Where, according to Walter, are he and his family going on their next trip?

   （根據華特的想法，他和家人下次應該去哪裡旅行？）

   (A) Back to Colorado

   (B) Texas

   (C) Wyoming

   (D) Australia

   Answer: (C)

5. Express Feelings
表達感覺

a. Thanks
感謝

Rhonda had lent Joey a large sum of money, which Joey paid back as soon as he could. He had needed the money because he had lost in a gambling game, and he owed the other players quite a bit. Joey found Rhonda later and gave her back the original sum plus ten percent.

"I added ten percent to the original sum to show you how much I appreciate your helping me," Joey told her.

"It was the least I could do. You were in trouble, so I bailed you out. No big deal."

"Well, it certainly shows me how much of a friend you are. Thank you so much. I really owe you."

中譯

蘭達借了一大筆錢給喬依，喬依盡早將錢歸還。他需要那筆錢是因為他賭博輸了錢，欠別人一大筆賭債。喬依後來去找蘭達，將錢全數歸還，並多加了本金的百分之十。

「我另外加了百分之十，是為了要表示妳對我協助的無上謝意。」喬依告訴她。

「那是我至少能夠做到的。你有麻煩，我幫你脫困，不用客氣。」

「嗯，那讓我知道妳是一個多好的朋友。真的很感謝妳，我會記得妳的恩惠。」

Questions:

1. How did Joey lose a large sum of money?

    （喬依為何損失一大筆錢？）

    (A) It was stolen

    (B) He gambled it away

    (C) He misplaced it

    (D) He made a poor investment

    Answer: (B)

2. What did Joey do to show his thanks?

    （喬依如何表達他的謝意？）

    (A) He gave Rhonda a hug

    (B) He gave Rhonda a present

    (C) He kissed Rhonda

    (D) He gave her back 10 percent more than he owed

    Answer: (D)

Dialogue:

Joey: Thank you so much.
（非常感謝妳。）

Rhonda: It was nothing.
（沒什麼。）

Joey: No, it wasn't.
（不，不是這樣的。）

Not just anybody would lend me that much money.
（不是任何人都願意借我那麼一大筆錢。）

You're a real friend.
（妳是一個真正的朋友。）

Rhonda: Well, that is what friends are for.
（哎，那是朋友該做的。）

Questions:

1. **What does Joey call Rhonda?**

    （喬依稱蘭達什麼？）

    (A) A pretty woman

    (B) A slut

    (C) A real friend

    (D) A champion

    Answer: (C)

2. **What does Rhonda compare her favor to?**

    （蘭達把她的善意比喻為什麼？）

    (A) Nothing impressive

    (B) Climbing Mt. Everest

    (C) Flying to the moon

    (D) Seeing the world

    Answer: (A)

b. Anger
生氣

MP3-19

5

Express Feelings 表達感覺

"I can't believe you'd sleep with my girlfriend!" Thomas said to Billy. Thomas' face was bright red. His hands were balled into fists, and it was all he could do not to slam them into Billy's face.

"It was a mistake," Billy replied.

Thomas couldn't hold himself back now. He would have launched at Billy and strangled him if it hadn't been for the fact that his girlfriend had just entered the room. The moment became overwhelming for Thomas; both his girlfriend and his best friend, the people who had slept together, were in the room. Thomas fainted.

中譯

　　「我真無法相信你竟然和我女朋友上床！」湯馬斯對比利說。湯馬斯的臉一陣赤紅。他的雙拳緊握，那是他唯一能控制自己不賞比利幾個巴掌的方法。

「那是個誤會，」比利回答。

湯馬斯再也不能控制自己了。要不是他女朋友剛好走進房裡，他隨時會衝向比利，把他勒死。他的女朋友和最好的朋友，兩個人上床了，此時還同時出現在房間裡；這一刻真讓湯馬斯完全不能支持，於是湯馬斯昏了過去。

Questions:

1. Why was Thomas upset with Billy?

（湯馬斯為了何事對比利不滿？）

(A) Billy stole his CDs

(B) Billy slept with Thomas' girlfriend

(C) Billy hit him

(D) Billy forgot to buy him a ham sandwich

Answer: (B)

2. What color was Thomas's face?

（湯馬斯的臉上呈現什麼顏色？）

(A) Red

(B) White

(C) Blue

(D) Green

Answer: (A)

Conversation:

Thomas: I can't believe you'd sleep with my girlfriend!
（我無法相信你和我女友上床！）

Billy: Look. It was a mistake!
（聽好。這是個誤會！）

We were both drunk.
（我們兩人都喝醉了。）

Thomas: A mistake? I could kill you for this mistake!
（誤會？我會為了這個誤會宰了你！）

Billy: I'm sorry. What else do you want me to do?

（對不起。你到底要我怎麼做？）

Thomas: Get out of here before I kill you.

（在我殺了你之前滾出去。）

Questions:

1. What reason does Billy give for his actions?

（比利對他的行為有何說詞？）

(A) It was late and he was tired

(B) He didn't realize Gina was Thomas' girlfriend

(C) They were both drunk

(D) He mistook her for someone else

Answer: (C)

2. What does Billy call his action?

（比利說他的行為是什麼？）

(A) An accident

(B) A mistake

(C) An enjoyable experience

(D) A rare occurrence

Answer: (B)

c. Excitement
興奮

MP3-20

As far back as Tina could remember, she had wanted to go to a Pearl Jam concert. So when her boyfriend, Freddy, came by and told her they were playing in Dallas and that he had bought tickets for the two of them, Tina was overwhelmed. She jumped up and down, skipped across the room, and hugged her boyfriend in excitement.

"I can't believe it!" she exclaimed. She rushed over to the phone to call all of her friends and tell them what a great boyfriend she had.

中譯

就提娜所能記憶，她一直想要去看「珍珠果醬」的演唱會。因此，當她的男朋友弗瑞迪來找她，並告訴她有關「珍珠果醬」在達拉斯表演的消息，而且他還為兩人買好票時，提娜高興極了。她上上下下地跳著，在室內跑來跑去，並且興奮難抑地抱住了她的男朋友。

「真是太難相信了！」她喊叫著。她急急拿起電話打給她的朋友們，並告訴他們，她的男朋友有多棒。

Questions:

1. Which band are they going to see?

   （他們要去看哪個樂團的表演？）

   (A) Alice in Chains

   (B) Pearl Jam

   (C) Ace of Bass

   (D) Dave Matthews Band

   Answer: (B)

2. How did Tina react to the news?

   （提娜對這個消息的反應如何？）

   (A) With excitement

   (B) With despair

   (C) With sadness

   (D) With lack of interest

   Answer: (A)

Conversation:

Tina: I can't believe you got me tickets to the Pearl Jam concert!

（真是無法相信你為我買了「珍珠果醬」演唱會的票！）

Freddy: Well, I knew they were your favorite band.

（哪，我知道他們是妳最喜愛的樂團。）

When I saw their show advertised in the newspaper, I had to get you tickets.

（當我在報上見到他們的演出宣傳時，我就一定要為妳弄到票。）

Tina: You are the coolest boyfriend ever.

（你真是最酷的男朋友了。）

Freddy: What can I say?

（我還能說什麼？）

Questions:

1. Where did Freddy see an advertisement for the Pearl Jam concert?

   （弗瑞迪在哪裡見到「珍珠果醬」演唱會的宣傳？）

   (A) On the internet

   (B) On a bulletin board

   (C) On a flyer placed on his windshield

   (D) In the newspaper

   Answer: (D)

2. Why did Tina get so excited about the concert?

   （提娜為什麼對這個演唱會感到這麼興奮？）

   (A) She likes rock concerts

   (B) Pearl Jam is her favorite band

   (C) Freddy never buys her things

   (D) She wasn't excited about the concert

   Answer: (B)

d. Sorry
歉疚

MP3-21

After Joe got in a fight with Rose because they couldn't agree what kind of car he should buy, he felt bad. There was no real point to the fight. He was just tired and frustrated from work. He sat in the coffee shop, thinking about the fight. He decided to call Rose and apologize. He had taken his frustrations out on and felt that she didn't deserve that kind of treatment.

中譯

　　因為兩人對應該買什麼樣的車，意見不同，使得喬和蘿絲吵了一架，喬為此感到很難過。這個架吵得實在沒有來由，他只是因為工作勞累而沮喪。他坐在咖啡店，想著這次兩人的口角，他決定要去向蘿絲道歉。他把他的挫折感發洩在蘿絲身上，而且覺得她不應該受到這樣的對待。

Questions:

1. What did Joe and Rose get in a fight about?

   （喬和蘿絲吵架的原因是什麼？）

   (A) Joe had lost money while gambling

   (B) Rose had cheated on him

   (C) Joe forget Rose's birthday

   (D) Rose disagreed on what kind of car he should buy

   Answer: (D)

2. Where was Joe when he was thinking about apologizing?

   （喬想到要向蘿絲道歉時，人在哪裡？）

   (A) In the coffee shop

   (B) In his room

   (C) At the library

   (D) At his parents' house

   Answer: (A)

Dialogue:

Joe: I'm real sorry about getting upset with you earlier.
（我很抱歉剛剛不該和妳生氣。）

Rose: Hmph. I'm sure you are.
（哼！你當然抱歉了。）

Joe: I really am.
（是真的。）

It's just that I've been having a lot of stress at work.
（我的工作壓力太大了。）

Rose: Whatever.
（隨你怎麼講。）

Joe: Please accept my apology.
（請接受我的道歉。）

I'll make it up to you.
（我會補償妳的。）

I'll take you to your favorite restaurant, Roy's Cafeteria Italiana.
（我請妳去妳最喜歡的餐廳 —— 羅伊義大利自助餐廳。）

Rose: You will?
（你會？）

I mean, I'll think about it.
（我是說，我會考慮考慮。）

Questions:

1. Where did Joe offer to take Rose?

    （喬要請蘿絲去哪裡？）

    (A) Walter's Cafeteria Espana

    (B) Roy's Cafeteria Italiana

    (C) McDonald's

    (D) Luck o' the Irish Restaurant

    Answer: (B)

2. What is the source of Joe's anger?

    （喬的憤怒來源是什麼？）

    (A) Rose

    (B) His golf game

    (C) Work

    (D) His car keeps breaking down

    Answer: (C)

e. Embarrassed
感到尷尬

MP3-22

Lester didn't know that his swimsuit had been pulled off by the tide. When he got out of the water and onto the beach, he realized what had happened when he saw everybody staring at him. He froze and his face turned red. A few girls were nearby and they shouted out a few rude comments. Finally, he decided to run over to his beach towel and cover himself with it. He had never been so embarrassed in his entire life.

中譯

　　李斯特並不知道泳褲被海浪沖脫了。當他離開水面走上海灘，每個人都盯著他看時，他才知道發生什麼事。他一下子僵住了，臉上一陣紅。附近有幾個女孩子，她們為此大聲喊著無禮的閒話。終於，他決定跑向他的海灘浴巾，並將自己包起來。他的一生中從來沒有這麼尷尬過。

Questions:

1. What did the tide pull off of Lester?

    （海浪沖脫了李斯特的什麼東西？）

    (A) His swimsuit

    (B) His watch

    (C) His toupee

    (D) His glasses

    Answer: (A)

2. What does Lester decide to use to cover himself?

    （李斯特決定用什麼把自己包起來？）

    (A) His friend's extra bikini

    (B) His towel

    (C) His hands

    (D) His swimsuit

    Answer: (B)

Dialogue:

Lester: Hey, Jimmy, could you grab me a towel?
（嘿，吉米，你能拿條浴巾給我吧？）

Jimmy: What for, Lester?
（李斯特，為什麼？）

Lester: Well, my, uh…
（哎，我，呃……）

Jimmy: What? I can't hear you! Speak up!
（什麼？我聽不到！大聲點兒！）

Lester: My swimsuit fell off!
（我的泳褲掉了！）

Jimmy: Well then, how much will you pay me to bring you a towel?
（即然如此，拿浴巾給你，你要付我多少錢？）

Lester: Just bring me a towel, or I'll tell Mom.
（快拿條浴巾給我，不然我就告訴媽。）

Questions:

1. What did Lester ask Jimmy to bring him?

（李斯特要吉米拿什麼東西給他？）

(A) A beer

(B) A towel

(C) A raft

(D) A volleyball

Answer: (B)

2. Who did Lester threaten to tell?

（李斯特威脅要向誰告狀？）

(A) Mom

(B) Dad

(C) Their sister

(D) Jimmy's girlfriend

Answer: (A)

f. Complaining
抱怨

MP3-23

Alex had taken his son, Andrew, to the Grand Canyon, hoping that they could spend some quality father and son time together so that he could get to know his son. Instead, Alex found himself wishing that they had never gone on the trip together. Every five minutes, Andrew found something new to complain about, whether it was rocks in his shoes, blisters on his feet, or the hot weather. After three hours of Andrew's complaining, Alex was ready to tie Andrew to a tree and leave him there. He finally turned around and scolded the boy, telling him that nobody likes a complainer! Silence followed through most of the trip.

中譯

　　亞歷克斯帶他的兒子安德魯到大峽谷，希望他們能好好共度一些美好的父子時光，以便多了解他的兒子。

但相反地，亞歷克斯卻希望他們從來沒有一起進行這次
旅行。每隔五分鐘，安德魯總能找到一個新的抱怨理由，
要不是鞋子裡有石頭、腳上長水泡，就是天氣太炎熱。
安德魯抱怨了三個小時候，亞歷克斯幾乎想把安德魯綁
在樹上，讓他獨自留在那兒。他終於回頭責備這個男孩，
明白地告訴他沒有人會喜歡一個喋喋抱怨的人。結果，
沈默幾乎伴隨了他們大半的旅程。

Questions:

1. What did Alex hate about Andrew?

（亞歷克斯討厭安德魯什麼？）

(A) The color of his hair

(B) His constant complaining

(C) His bitterness

(D) His obsession with ants

Answer: (B)

2.　Where did Alex take his son?

（亞歷克斯帶他兒子去哪裡？）

(A) To see Ole Faithful

(B) To New York

(C) To the Grand Canyon

(D) To Niagara Falls

Answer: (C)

Dialogue:

Andrew: I've got rocks in my shoes.
（我的鞋子裡有石頭。）

Can we stop?
（我們可以停一下嗎？）

Alex:　Why do you think you have rocks in your shoes?
（你為什麼認為你的鞋子裡有石頭？）

Andrew: Because I can feel them.
（因為我可以感覺得到。）

I wouldn't be complaining if I didn't feel them.
（要不是我感覺到了，我才不會抱怨。）

Alex: It seems like you feel a lot of stuff.
（看來你老是可以感覺到許多東西。）

You haven't shut up since we started hiking.
（你從健行一開始就沒閉過嘴。）

Andrew: Well, a lot of stuff is bugging me.
（哎呀，許多事可煩得很。）

Like the rocks in my shoes!
（就像鞋子裡的石頭！）

Alex: Look, Andrew. Nobody likes a whiner.
（安德魯，聽仔細了。沒有人喜歡沒事哀哀喳喳的人。）

Every word you've said since we started has been a complaint.
（從一開始，你說的每個字都是抱怨。）

Andrew: Yeah, well, can we stop?
（是呀，但我們可以停一會兒嗎？）

Questions:

1. **What did Alex call Andrew?**

   （亞歷克斯叫安德魯什麼？）

   (A) A robber

   (B) A culinary artist

   (C) A whiner

   (D) A little kid

   Answer: (C)

2. **What is Andrew's problem?**

   （困擾安德魯的是什麼？）

   (A) He's afraid of heights

   (B) He's tired

   (C) He's too hot

   (D) He has rocks in his shoes

   Answer: (D)

g. Disappointment
失望

5

Express Feelings 表達感覺

When Tina found out that the Pearl Jam concert was cancelled, she was overwhelmed with disappointment. She became extremely depressed. Freddy tried to cheer her up. He took her to her favorite club, Il Duce, and he took her to her favorite restaurant, Jazz. He even took her to see her family. It seemed this Pearl Jam concert really meant a lot to her, and nothing was going to cheer her up. When Freddy finally asked her what was wrong, she replied, "I'm getting used to being disappointed."

After a few weeks, Tina finally reverted back to her original, happy self, completely surprising Freddy.

中譯

提娜得知「珍珠果醬」的演唱會取消時，她實在覺得太失望了。她還因此變得極為沮喪。弗瑞迪試著激勵

她。他帶她去她喜歡的「元首夜總會」，還帶她到她最喜歡的「爵士餐廳」。他甚至帶她去探望她的家人。「珍珠果醬」這件事似乎對她真的意義深重，什麼事也鼓舞不了她。最後，弗瑞迪問她到底出了什麼問題，她回答，「我已經逐漸習慣失望了。」

幾週後，提娜終於又恢復她原有的快樂本性，這倒是讓弗瑞迪感到有些驚訝。

Questions:

1.　**Why was Tina disappointed?**

（提娜為何感到失望？）

(A) She found out Freddy was unfaithful

(B) Her dad never showed up at her volleyball games

(C) The Pearl Jam concert was cancelled

(D) The people who were working for her were late with their reports

Answer: (C)

2. Which was Tina's favorite club?

（提娜最喜歡的夜總會是哪一個？）

(A) Il Duce

(B) Jazz

(C) The Underground

(D) Inferno

Answer: (A)

Dialogue:

Freddy: So why the sudden turnaround?

（怎麼會有這麼大的轉變？）

You were depressed about Pearl Jam for two weeks and now you're happy again? What's the deal?

（妳原本因為「珍珠果醬」而沮喪了二週，現在妳又快樂起來了？到底怎怎麼回事？）

Tina: I just realized it was a little silly to be so disappointed about one concert.

（我發現為了一個演唱會這麼失望有點好笑。）

I'm sure I'll get another chance.
（我一定還有機會去參加的。）

Freddy: That's true.
（那倒是真的。）

I'm glad you came to your senses.
（我很高興妳能領悟過來。）

Tina: Now you can take me out to eat.
（你可以帶我出去吃飯了。）

Freddy: Where do you want to eat?
（妳想去哪裡吃飯？）

Tina: Mac Donald's.
（麥當勞。）

You always know what you're going to get, so you're never disappointed.
（妳總是知道妳想去哪吃飯，所之妳從來不會為吃飯的事失望。）

Freddy: I guess you never got used to disappointment.
（我想你大概從來沒有習慣於失望吧。）

Questions:

1. Where are they going to go eat?

   （他們要去哪兒吃飯？）

   (A) Burger King

   (B) MacDonald's

   (C) Razzo's

   (D) Jazz

   Answer: (B)

2. Why did Tina stop being depressed about the Pearl Jam concert?

   （提娜為何不再為「珍珠果醬」取消的事感到沮喪？）

   (A) She realized there were more important things to worry about

   (B) She realized it was silly to be depressed about a concert

   (C) She won the lottery

   (D) She just had a baby and she forgot about the concert

   Answer: (B)

h. Fear
恐懼

Lila was sitting in her room at the hospital. Her eyes had a moist tint to them, as though she had been crying recently, but she wasn't crying now, perhaps she was out of tears, or her pride was too strong to show her fear before her family. Flowers lined the tables on each side of her; each vase was brought in one at a time by friends and family members as each one paid their respects. Each flower reminded her of why she was there: to see how long she had left to live.

Socrates once advised Plato to not fear death, for we don't know what death brings. Lila, though, at this point, was unable to heed that advice. Looking deep into her eyes, her husband, Joel, could see her fear, and feeling her hand squeezing his, he could feel her fear, no matter how

much she tried to hide it.

中譯

　　莉拉坐在醫院的病房中。她的眼睛有些濕濡，彷彿她才剛哭過，但她現在並沒有在哭泣，也許她是欲哭無淚了，或者她的自尊強到讓她不願在家人面前顯示恐懼。她兩旁的桌上都擺滿了鮮花，每個花瓶都是她朋友和家人來向她告別的時候帶來的。每一朵花都讓她想到她為何在這裡，讓她明確地知道她還能活多久。

　　蘇格拉底有次告訴柏拉圖對死亡不要有恐懼，因為我們不知道死亡會帶來什麼，但莉拉在這個節骨眼兒無法留意這個忠告。在她的眼睛深處，她的丈夫，喬，見到了她的恐懼，並感到她的手用力地抓擰著他的手，不論她如何藏匿，他感覺到了她的恐懼。

Questions:

1. What did Lila's family give to her?

（莉拉的家人給她什麼？）

(A) Candy

(B) Gold

(C) Flowers

(D) Incense

Answer: (C)

2. Who did Socrates advise about death?

（蘇格拉底對誰做了死亡的忠告？？）

(A) Aristotle

(B) Plato

(C) Aristophanes

(D) Alexander

Answer: (B)

Dialogue:

Lila: So, Doctor, what is the verdict?
（醫生，你的裁決是什麼？）

Doctor: Lila, I know you've been living in much fear.
（莉拉，我知道妳一直活在恐懼之中。）

You have got to give yourself some hope.
（妳得給自己一些希望。）

Lila: But is there any hope?
（還有希望嗎？）

Doctor: It would appear that the treatment has been working and the cancer is receding.
（看來這個療法有了功效，癌細胞正逐漸減少。）

Lila: Does that mean I have longer than three weeks to live?
（那表示我不止只能活三週？）

Doctor: That means you might live a full life.
（那表示妳可能可以長壽。）

Questions:

1. How long did the doctor originally think Lila had to live?

（醫生原來認為莉拉只能活多久？）

(A) One week

(B) Two weeks

(C) Three weeks

(D) Four weeks

Answer: (C)

2. What was Lila diagnosed with?

（莉拉診斷出來的是什麼？）

(A) AIDS

(B) Syphilis

(C) Tapeworms

(D) Cancer

Answer: (D)

6. Talking about Events
談論事件

a. Something happened before
過去發生的事

MP3-26

Rodney and Joey were at a coffee shop, sitting in the corner, sipping on their café lattes and watching all the people around them.

"So are you and Jessica still going out?" Joey asked Rodney idly.

"Nope, she's not my girlfriend anymore," Rodney answered.

"What happened?"

"Well, when I was going over to her place to pick her up to go out to the movies, there was a guy there. I mean,

not there, but he was leaving when I was coming and we passed each other on the walkway up to her door. I asked her who that was and she wouldn't tell me. She dismissed my concern and told me that she had to go get ready. Next thing I know, she comes back and tells me that we should take a break."

"Then what?"

"Well, I told her that I wasn't going to take any breaks. It was all or nothing."

"And?"

"She decided it was nothing. I guess apparently she wanted to take a break with that guy who I had passed. I imagine she's going out with him now."

羅尼跟喬伊坐在咖啡店的角落，邊喝拿鐵咖啡，邊觀察周圍的人。

「你還在跟潔西卡約會嗎？」喬伊懶懶地問羅尼。

「沒有。她再也不是我女朋友了。」羅尼回道。

「發生什麼事了？」

「喔，我去她家接她看電影時，有一個男的在那裡。也不能說在那裡，那個男的剛好要離開，而我正好去，我們兩個在她家門前的走道擦身而過。我問她，那是誰，她不願告訴我。她不理我的詢問，告訴我她得準備出門。接著，她又回來告訴我，我們應該暫時分開。」

「然後呢？」

「我跟她說我不要分開。不是在一起就是分手。」

「接著？」

「她決意分手。我猜很顯然地，她想跟我分手，是為了與那個和我擦身而過的男人在一起。我想她現在正跟他在交往中。」

Questions:

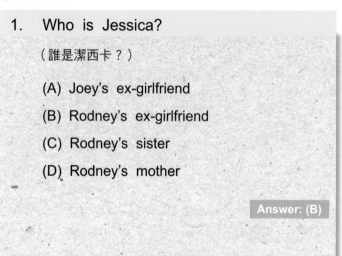

1. Who is Jessica?

   （誰是潔西卡？）

   (A) Joey's ex-girlfriend
   (B) Rodney's ex-girlfriend
   (C) Rodney's sister
   (D) Rodney's mother

   Answer: (B)

2. Jessica had originally wanted to do what with Rodney?

   （潔西卡原本要與羅尼做什麼？）

   (A) Take a break
   (B) Break up
   (C) Go to the movies
   (D) Go to a concert

   Answer: (A)

Conversation:

Rodney: So, what about you?
（那你怎樣？）

Are you still going out with Rebecca?
（還在跟露貝卡交往嗎？）

Joey: Nope, same kind of thing happened.
（沒有，發生了同樣的事。）

Rodney: Really?
（真的？）

Joey: She immediately broke it off with me.
（她立刻和我分手了。）

Rodney: Why'd she do that?
（她為何這麼做？）

Joey: She found out that I was seeing Melissa on the side.
（她發現我同時與梅麗沙交往。）

Rodney: So you had it coming, eh?
（所以是你的緣故？）

Joey: Guess I did.
（沒錯。）

Questions:

1. Who was Joey seeing on the side?

    （喬伊同時與誰約會？）

    (A) Rebecca

    (B) Veronica

    (C) Melissa

    (D) Diane

    Answer: (C)

2. What did Rebecca do to Joey?

    （麗貝卡對喬伊做了什麼？）

    (A) She offered him a break

    (B) She cooked him pizza

    (C) She gave him flowers

    (D) She broke up with him

    Answer: (D)

b. An activity
活動

MP3-27

Mrs. Johnson took her place at the head of the classroom. She looked out at all of her students until they became silent and at attention. "Good morning class," she said to them.

"Good morning Mrs. Johnson," they replied.

"For today's activity, we have a coloring book for you all to do. But instead of coloring the pictures in, you're going to cut out the shapes from colored paper and glue them onto your page."

She gave the colored paper to one child, Johnny, to pass out to the class, and she passed out the coloring sheets herself.

6

Talking about Events 談論事件

129

中譯

　　強森太太站在教室前面。她注視全班學生直到他們安靜、專心。「早安，班上同學。」

　　「早安，強森太太。」全班回答道。

　　「今天的活動是要你們大家做一本彩色的書，但不要你們將圖片著色，我要你們從色紙剪下各種形狀，然後把它們貼到紙上。」

　　她將色紙交給一個叫強尼的孩子，讓他把色紙發給全班。而她自己則負責發圖畫紙。

Questions:

1. What is the activity?

   （他們做什麼活動？）

   (A) Cutting and pasting shapes

   (B) Coloring in pictures

   (C) Hoola-hoops

   (D) Running around in circles

   Answer: (A)

2. Which student helped pass out supplies?

   （哪位學生幫忙發用具？）

   (A) Mike

   (B) Donald

   (C) Johnny

   (D) Rebecca

   Answer: (C)

6 Talking about Events 談論事件

Conversation:

Mrs. Johnson: You're doing well, Mike.
（麥克，你做得很好。）

Mike: Thank you, Mrs. Johnson.
（謝謝，強森太太。）

Mrs. Johnson: I like you choice of colors. That blue goes really well with that red.
（我喜歡你選的顏色。那藍色真的很配那個紅色。）

Mike: Thank you, Mrs. Johnson. My dad always said that I've got a good eye for things.
He thinks I should be an artist.
（謝謝，強森太太。我爸爸常說我對事物的眼光很好。他覺得我應該做藝術家。）

Mrs. Johnson: What do you think? Do you want to be an artist when you grow up?
（那你認為呢？你長大後想成為藝術家嗎？）

Mike: I think that would be neat.
（我想那是個好主意。）

Questions:

1. Which color goes really well with the red?

   （什麼顏色跟紅色搭配得很好？）

   (A) Yellow

   (B) Green

   (C) Orange

   (D) Blue

   Answer: (D)

2. What does Mrs. Johnson think Mike should be when he grows up?

   （強森太太認為麥克長大應該可以做什麼？）

   (A) An artist

   (B) An engineer

   (C) A trash collector

   (D) A musician

   Answer: (A)

6 Talking about Events 談論事件

c. An event
事件

MP3-28

The Scottish festival began the day before, but Donnie had to work, so he couldn't go. It was going on through the weekend, however, and on this day, Donnie could be found there. He was skimming through the people, looking for someone he knew, when he remembered that Veronica mentioned she would like to go. He pulled out his cell phone and called her.

"Hey Veronica. Are you going to come to the festival?" Donnie asked as he dodged a person coming out of a vendor's tent. "Well, when do you think you'll get there?" Donnie used the word "there" to make it sound as though he thought about her before going himself.

前天，蘇格蘭節開始，東尼有工作不能參加，不過節慶將持續到週末。這天，在哪兒可以找到東尼。他穿過人群，尋找認識的人。想到凡尼卡說過她想來，他拿起手機，打給她。

「嗨！凡尼卡。你要來參加節慶嗎？」他邊問邊躲開一個從小販營帳出來的人。「你什麼時候會到那兒？」東尼用「那兒」的字眼，以便聽起來彷彿他在去之前就想到她。

Questions:

1.   What kind of festival is it?

（這是什樣的節慶？）

(A) A food tasting festival

(B) An Irish festival

(C) A Scottish festival

(D) A music festival

Answer: (C)

2.   When was the festival going on?

（何時舉行節慶？）

(A) One day only

(B) All weekend

(C) Two days during the week

(D) None of the above

Answer: (B)

Conversation:

Donnie: Hey Veronica.

Are you going to go to the festival?

（嗨！凡尼卡。你要去參加節慶嗎？）

Veronica: Yeah, I was thinking about it, if I could find someone to go with.

（是啊，如果我找到人跟我去的話，我會考慮。）

Donnie: I'll go with you, just meet me there. What time do you think you can make it?

（我可以跟你去，我們在那兒碰面。你何時會到？）

Veronica: In 45 minutes.

（45 分鐘內。）

What are all those people I can hear?

（電話中可以聽到很多人在説話，是誰？）

You're already there, aren't you?

（你已經到了是不是？）

Donnie: Yes, actually I am.

（沒錯。）

Veronica: What's it like?

（怎麼樣？）

Donnie: It's pretty fun.
（挺有趣的。）

There are lots of different crafts and food vendors.
（有許多特別的工藝品，還有小販。）

The Scotch eggs are excellent here.
（蘇格蘭煎蛋很好吃。）

You should come out quick.
（你該快一點來。）

Questions:

1. What item does Donnie think is excellent?

（東尼覺得什麼很棒？）

(A) Guinness

(B) Whiskey

(C) Turkey legs

(D) Scotch eggs

Answer: (D)

2. When can Veronica get there?

（凡尼卡何時會到？）

(A) 10 minutes

(B) 20 minutes

(C) 30 minutes

(D) 45 minutes

Answer: (D)

6

Talking about Events 談論事件

d. Ed bought a new car
艾德買了部新車

Ed pulled up in his new car, still shining from the fresh clean and tune-up that it received at the car lot. He looked at the black Toyota Camry and called his friend, Jill. "Guess what I just got," Ed said into his cell phone.

"What's that?" Jill replied.

"A new car!"

"What kind is it?"

"A Toyota Camry 2004. It's all black. It's got a gray interior, a CD player, fully loaded, an alarm it's awesome. Where are you right now? I'll show you."

"I'm over at Lisa's place. Come by and show us all."

"I'll be right there."

　　艾德停下他乾淨、完好一如剛從停車場接收，依然光芒四射的新車。他看著黑色的 Toyota　Camry，隨即打電話給他的朋友，吉爾。

　　「猜猜我剛拿到什麼？」艾德對著手機講。

　　「是什麼？」吉爾問。

　　「一輛新車！」

　　「哪一種？」

　　「2004 出產的 Toyota　Camry。全黑，內部是灰色，有光碟機，裡面有滿滿的 CD，還有鬧鐘。很棒！你現在在哪兒？我秀給你看。」

　　「我在麗沙家，你過來秀給我們看。」

　　「我馬上到。」

Questions:

1. Where is Jill?

（吉爾在哪兒？）

(A) At her place

(B) At Joey's place

(C) At the store

(D) At Lisa's place

Answer: (D)

2. What kind of car did Ed buy?

（艾德買了哪種車？）

(A) Honda Accord

(B) Toyota Camry

(C) Ford Taurus

(D) Mercury Sable

Answer: (B)

Conversation:

Ed: So what do you think of it?
（你覺得如何？）

Jill: It's nice.
It's very comfortable too.
Can I take it for a spin?
（很棒，也很舒適。我可以開它繞一繞嗎？）

Ed: I don't see why not.
Here's the keys.
（有何不可，鑰匙給你。）

Jill: It's a smooth drive, too.
I wish I had this car.
（開起來很順，我希望有這樣的車。）

Ed: So, what do you like most about it?
（你最喜歡它那一點？）

Jill: The sound system, definitely.
（絕對是它的音響系統。）

6

Talking about Events 談論事件

Questions:

1. What is Jill's favorite thing about the car?

    （吉爾最喜歡這輛車哪一點？）

    (A) Its smoothness

    (B) Its comfort

    (C) Its sound system

    (D) Its color

    Answer: (C)

2. What does Jill ask to do with the car?

    （吉爾對車子做什麼要求？）

    (A) Look at it

    (B) Sit in it

    (C) Sleep in it

    (D) Drive it

    Answer: (D)

7. Need Help
需要幫忙

a. At class
在課堂上

Throughout the Physics lecture, Simon was staring at the wall behind the professor. Halfway through, he had lost complete understanding of what the professor was talking about. For a while, he looked around at all the other students to see if they were in the same boat, but it seemed that he was the only one that was utterly confused. He needed some help.

After class, he went over to his friend, Laura, who he knew to make good grades on everything. "Hey Laura," he greeted her.

"Hey Simon," she replied.

"Do you think maybe you could help

me on the assignment? I'm totally lost," Simon said sheepishly.

"Yeah, sure, no problem. When do you want to meet to go over it?"

"I was thinking about meeting on Thursday night? Is that cool?"

"Sure."

中譯

　　整堂物理課，賽門都盯著教授身後的牆。課上到一半，他已經完全聽不懂教授在說什麼。他觀察周圍的同學一會兒，想知道他們是否也一樣。但似乎只有他聽不懂。他需要幫忙。

　　下課後，他跑去找朋友蘿拉。據他所知她每科成績都很好。「嗨！蘿拉。」他向她打招呼。

　　「嗨！賽門。」她回道。

　　「你可以幫我一些作業上的忙嗎？我完全不懂。」賽門不好意思問道。

　　「喔。當然，沒問題。你想要何時碰面來討論作業？」

　　「星期四晚上碰面，可以嗎？」

　　「沒問題。」

Questions:

1. Which class did Simon need help in?

   （賽門需要幫忙的是哪門課？）

   (A) Marketing Management

   (B) Calculus

   (C) Physics

   (D) Operations Management

   Answer: (C)

2. When are Simon and Laura going to meet?

   （賽門和蘿拉何時要碰面？）

   (A) Friday

   (B) Thursday

   (C) Wednesday

   (D) Tuesday

   Answer: (B)

Conversation:

Simon: Could you help me with the assignment?
（作業你可以幫我嗎？）

Laura: Sure. When do you want to meet?
（可以。你想何時碰面？）

Simon: I was thinking Thursday night after class, over at the Imperial Coffee café that's right next to campus.
（我想星期四晚上下課後，到學校旁邊的帝王咖啡廳。）

Laura: Sounds good.
（聽起來不錯。）

You're going to have to buy me a mocha, though.
（但是，你要請我喝杯摩卡喔。）

Simon: Hey, if you help me pass this class, I'll buy you anything.
（嘿，你要是幫我通過這門課，我什麼都可以買給妳。）

Laura: I'm going to stick you to your word.
（我會讓你守住諾言。）

Questions:

1. Where are Laura and Simon going to meet?

    （他們要在哪兒碰面？）

    (A) Java Dave's

    (B) Imperial Coffee

    (C) Marbuck's

    (D) Fusion Coffee

    Answer: (B)

2. What does Laura say that Simon has to buy her?

    （羅拉要賽門買給她什麼？）

    (A) Chai tea

    (B) Boba tea

    (C) Mocha

    (D) Latte

    Answer: (C)

b. At the airport
在飛機場

MP3-31

Fred was dropped off at the airport by his friend Walter. He looked around the terminal and couldn't figure out where to go to get to his flight to Paris on International Air, so he scanned around, looking for someone that he could ask for directions. There were a lot of military personnel around, toting large automatic assault rifles – he wasn't too keen on asking them. There were people from the crowd, all running about and obviously rushed. Finally, he found a desk with a line. The line was extensive, and he couldn't quite figure out what the desk was for, but he went ahead and got in the line.

中譯

　　佛瑞得的朋友瓦特載他到機場。他看看航站四周搞不清楚要到哪兒搭國際航空到巴黎的班機。他四處看看，想找可以問路的人。附近有許多軍人背著大型自動攻擊來福槍。他不太想問他們。人群中有些人匆忙地跑著，顯然在趕時間。最後，他找到一個櫃檯，櫃臺前有人在排隊。隊伍排得很長，他不太清楚那個櫃檯是做什麼的，但他往前走加入了隊伍。

Questions:

1. Where was Fred going?

（佛瑞得要去哪兒？）

(A) Paris, France

(B) Moscow, Russia

(C) Geneva, Switzerland

(D) Munich, Germany

Answer: (A)

2. What were the military personnel holding?

（那些軍人身上帶著什麼？）

(A) Bags

(B) Assault rifles

(C) Pistols

(D) Machine guns

Answer: (B)

Conversation:

Fred: Is this the right line for the baggage check-in?
（這裡是行李登記的地方嗎？）

Clerk: No, this is the information desk.
（不，這裡是詢問處。）

Fred: Where is it?
（那麼在哪兒？）

Clerk: Which carrier are you using?
（你坐哪家航空公司？）

Fred: Delta.
（達美航空。）

Clerk: Follow the building down about a quarter of a mile and then turn left.
（沿著建築物走下去，大概走四分之一英里，再左轉。）

That's where the proper terminal is.
（那裡才是你要找的航站。）

Fred: Then what do I do?
（然後怎麼做？）

Clerk: Proceed to the security check point.
（繼續走過安全檢查站。）

Make sure you have your tickets on you.
（確定你帶著機票。）

Fred: Thanks.
（謝謝。）

Questions:

1. How far away is the baggage check in from where Fred is?

    （行李登記處距離佛瑞得有多遠？）

    (A) Quarter of a mile

    (B) Half a mile

    (C) One mile

    (D) Fifty feet

    Answer: (A)

2. Where does Fred go after the baggage check in?

    （佛瑞得行李登記後要前往哪裡？）

    (A) He goes onto the plane

    (B) He goes to the lobby

    (C) He goes to security

    (D) He goes to the ticket agent

    Answer: (C)

c. At the hotel
在旅館

MP3-32

Jake entered the Hotel Grande in San Antonio, marveling at the architecture of the lobby. It sure lived up to its name, Jake thought. He looked around to find the registration desk, where he could check in. He pulled aside a porter and asked where it was. "Right over there," the porter answered. "Do you need someone to take your bags?"

"No, I'm fine," Jake responded.

Jake went to the registration desk and said to the clerk: "I'd like a room please."

"For how long?" the clerk asked.

"For three nights. How much would that be?"

"What kind of bed?"

Jake thought for a moment, remembering how little he slept last time when he slept in a twin. "A queen sized bed, please."

"That will be 320 dollars. Do you have a credit card?" Jake handed her his credit card. "Good. Now if you need anything or have any questions, call the desk right here and we'll be glad to help you. Here is your key and enjoy your stay at Hotel Grande."

中譯

　　傑克走進聖安東尼歐的豪華飯店，驚嘆於大廳的建築。這飯店真是名符其實，傑克想。他四處尋找登記櫃檯，他拉住一位服務生詢問。「就在那兒，」服務生回答。「你需要人幫你提行李嗎？」

　　「不用了。我自己拿就行了。」傑克回道。

　　傑克走向登記櫃檯，向辦事員道：「請給我一間房間。」

　　「住多久？」辦事員問。

　　「三個晚上。多少錢？」

　　「哪種床？」

　　傑克想了一下，想到他上次睡單人床有多小。

　　「請給我雙人床。」

　　「總共是 320 美元。你有信用卡嗎？」

　　傑克遞給她信用卡。

　　「很好。假如有任何需要或任何問題，打電話到櫃檯，我們會樂於協助你。這是您的鑰匙，希望您在豪華飯店住得愉快。」

Questions:

1. How long will Jake be staying at the hotel?

（傑克要在這家飯店住多久？）

(A) 1 night

(B) 2 nights

(C) 3 nights

(D) 4 nights

Answer: (C)

2. What size of bed will Jake be sleeping in?

（傑克想睡多大的床？）

(A) Full

(B) Twin

(C) King

(D) Queen

Answer: (D)

Conversation:

Clerk: Hotel Grande, room service.
（豪華飯店，客房服務。）

How may I help you?
（有事嗎？）

Jake: Yeah, I need to get my sheets washed.
（嗯，我想要換洗床單。）

Clerk: We change them daily sir.
（我們每天都有換洗，先生。）

Jake: Oh, okay. Towels too?
（喔，好吧。毛巾也是嗎？）

Clerk: Any towel that you leave in the bath tub we will wash.
（你放在浴缸的每條毛巾我們都會洗過。）

Jake: Okay. How about a sandwich?
（那好，來一個三明治。）

Clerk: What kind of sandwich?
（哪種三明治？）

Jake: A ham sandwich.
（火腿三明治。）

Clerk: We'll bring it up to you sir.
（我們會送上去給您，先生。）

Questions:

1. How often do they change the sheets?

    （他們多久換床單？）

    (A) Once a visit
    (B) Every other day
    (C) Daily
    (D) Weekly

    Answer: (C)

2. What kind of sandwich did Jake order?

    （傑克點了什麼三明治？）

    (A) Turkey sandwich
    (B) Ham sandwich
    (C) Roast beef sandwich
    (D) Veggie sandwich

    Answer: (B)

d. At the cafeteria
在自助餐廳

MP3-33

Pete followed his friends into the cafeteria. They always ate there for lunch at school, even though Pete brought his own lunch. This day, though, he didn't bring his lunch and had to find a line to get into. He looked at the signs, which was where one would go to find help in a cafeteria, and found the line that held on the other end his pot of gold: fried chicken. The only thing in America that was more plentiful than lines and signs was grass. In some respect, it's a good thing because people always know where to go. Cafeterias, in that instance, are the true representative of America: they have a large diversity of foods and there are lots of lines and signs.

中譯

　　彼得跟著朋友進入自助餐廳。在學校,他們總是在這裡吃午餐,即使彼得自己有帶午餐。今天他沒帶午餐,必須找一個隊伍去排隊。他看著指示牌,在自助餐廳人們會在這兒尋求幫助。他發現他要的一鍋炸雞在另一邊的隊伍。在美國,唯一比排隊與指示牌多的只有草地。以某種觀點來看,這是件好事。因為人們會知道該往哪裡去。比如,自助餐廳就是美國真實的代表,裡面有各式各樣的食物,以及大排長龍的隊伍和指示牌。

Questions:

1. What did Pete want to eat for lunch?

   （彼得午餐想吃什麼？）

   (A) Fried chicken

   (B) Buffalo wings

   (C) Ham sandwich

   (D) Pizza

   Answer: (A)

2. In America, what are more plentiful than lines and signs?

   （在美國，什麼比隊伍和指示牌多？）

   (A) Trees

   (B) Pickup trucks

   (C) Grass

   (D) Ants

   Answer: (C)

Conversation:

Pete: I think I want some fried chicken today.
（我今天要吃炸雞。）

Mike: Not me, I'm in for pizza.
（我不要，我要吃披薩。）

That lines over there if you want to go with me.
（隊伍在那邊，假如你想跟我去的話。）

Pete: No, I'm pretty set on fried chicken.
（不，我很確定我要吃炸雞。）

Do you know where that line is?
（你知道隊伍在哪兒？）

Mike: Not really.
（我不清楚。）

Just look at all the signs above the lines.
（看看每個隊伍上面的指示牌吧。）

It's pretty self-explanatory.
（上面說明很清楚。）

Ah, I see it. The line is to the right of the sandwich line.
（啊，我看到了。是三明治右邊那一列。）

Pete: Right. I'll see you at the table.
（沒錯，我在餐桌等你。）

Questions:

1. Where is the line for fried chicken?

（炸雞的隊伍在哪兒？）

(A) To the left of the buffalo wings line

(B) To the right of the pizza line

(C) To the right of the sandwich line

(D) To the left of the turkey legs line

Answer: (C)

2. What is Mike going to eat for lunch?

（麥克中午要吃什麼？）

(A) Buffalo wings

(B) Pizza

(C) Sandwich

(D) Turkey leg

Answer: (B)

e. At the office
在公司

MP3-34

Michael was working on his Natchitoches Fried Chicken Company case when suddenly he came to a standstill. After a few moments of playing with his pencil and looking around his office for ideas, he decided he needed some help. He knew that he couldn't go straight to his supervisor for help, because if it was an easy solution, he would look like a fool, so he went over to his office buddy, John, across the hall.

"Hey John," Michael addressed him.

"Hey Mike. Need something?" John was obviously working on a project himself and he was deeply immersed in it. If it had been anyone else but Michael distracting him, he would have been angry.

"You busy? I need some help with

some figures."

"I guess I can help you some." John got up and followed Michael to his office.

中譯

麥可正著手納迪司炸雞公司的案子，突然他遇到了困難。他把玩著鉛筆一會兒、四處看看辦公室以引發靈感，最後他決定需要一點協助。他知道自己不能直接向上司尋求協助。因為假使很輕鬆就解決了，他就會像個傻瓜一樣。因此，他穿過走道走向他的工作伙伴，約翰。

「嗨！約翰。」麥可對他説。

「嗨！麥可。有事嗎？」約翰很明顯正著手一項方案，而且完全沈浸在其中。假如不是麥可而是別人來打擾他，他一定會生氣。

「你忙嗎？關於一些數字，我需要幫忙。」

「我可以幫你一點忙。」約翰起身跟著麥可到他的辦公室。

Questions:

1. Which company case was Michael working on?

（麥可正著手哪家公司的案子？）

(A) Tenaha Cheese Factory

(B) Revco Corporation

(C) Timpson and Smith's Nacho Company

(D) Natchitoches Fried Chicken Company

Answer: (D)

2. Where is John's office?

（約翰辦公室在哪兒？）

(A) Across the hall from Michael's

(B) One floor down from Michael's

(C) One floor up from Michael's

(D) In the building across the street

Answer: (A)

Conversation:

Michael: Could you help me out on some of these figures?
（你可以幫我解決這些數字嗎？）

John: Depends.　What are the figures for?
（看情形。這些數字是幹嘛？）

Michael: Ah, it's just some simple accounting stuff I need help with.
（啊，只是一些我需要人幫忙的簡單會計資料。）

I can't seem to make the balance sheet balance.
（我就是沒辦法使收支表平衡。）

John: I suppose I could take a look at it.
（我想我可以看一下。）

But I can't take longer than ten minutes, okay?
（但我最多只能花十分鐘，可以吧？）

Ten minutes is my limit, and after that I have to get back to work on my project, because it's due soon. Got it?
（十分鐘是我的極限，之後，我就要去忙我的方案，因為期限就快到了。瞭解嗎？）

Michael: Yeah sure. Hurry up, time's a wasting!
（當然。快點，別浪費時間！）

Questions:

1. What do Michael's figures concern?

   （麥可的數字是要做什麼？）

   (A) Income statements

   (B) Marketing statistics

   (C) Investment portfolio

   (D) Balance sheet

   Answer: (D)

2. How long does John allot to helping Michael?

   （約翰分配多少時間幫忙麥可？）

   (A) Ten minutes

   (B) Fifteen minutes

   (C) Twenty minutes

   (D) Thirty minutes

   Answer: (A)

8. Offering

提供

a. Offering drinks
供給飲料

MP3-35

Roger opened the door and in entered his evening guests, Lee and Brenda. Jeanette, Roger's wife, welcomed them in. "Have a seat," she said. After they were deep into their conversation, Jeanette said to her guests: "Where are my manners, I forgot to offer you two a drink. What would you like?"

"What do you have?" Lee asked.

Jeanette listed their beverage inventory.

"In that case, I'll have a Coke," Lee said.

"And I'll take a cosmo," Brenda added in.

"They'll be right up," Jeanette told them. She walked into the kitchen and a few moments later, returned with two drinks in her hand. "Roger, would you like anything?" she asked.

"Yeah, sure, I'll have a Scotch."

Jeanette went back into the kitchen and came out with Roger's drinks.

中譯

羅傑開門讓他今晚的客人，李和白蘭達進入。珍德，羅傑的太太將他們迎來。「請坐。」她說。談了良久之後，珍德對客人說：「我真沒禮貌。我竟然忘了請你們喝飲料。你們想喝什麼？」

「有什麼飲料？」李問。

珍德列舉了他們所有的飲料。

「這樣的話，我要可樂。」李說。

「我要卡摩。」白蘭德接著說。

　　「馬上好。」珍德跟他們說。她走進廚房，幾分鐘後，手上拿著兩杯飲料回來。「羅傑，你要喝點什麼嗎？」她問。

　　「好啊，我也來個蘇格蘭酒。」

　　珍德回到廚房，出來時拿著羅傑的飲料。

Questions:

1. What did Lee have to drink?

   （李喝什麼？）

   (A) Cosmo

   (B) Coke

   (C) Bourbon

   (D) Vodka tonic

   Answer: (B)

2. How many drinks did Jeanette have when she first came out of the kitchen?

   （珍德第一次從廚房出來時，拿了幾杯飲料？）

   (A) One

   (B) Two

   (C) Three

   (D) Four

   Answer: (B)

8 Offering 提供

Conversation:

Jeanette: So, how have you all been?
（你們最近過得如何？）

Brenda: We've been pretty good.
（我們很好。）

I heard you got a new job?
（聽說你找到新工作？）

Jeanette: Yes, it's for an accounting firm.
（是的，是家會計公司。）

Brenda: What do you do for them?
（你做什麼工作？）

Jeanette: Well, I work as an auditor.
（我是查帳人員。）

Oh, where are my manners?
（喔，我真沒禮貌。）

Can I get you two anything to drink?
（你們要喝什麼？）

Questions:

1. What is Jeanette's new job?

   （珍德的新工作是什麼？）

   (A) She's a writer

   (B) She's a newscaster

   (C) She's an auditor

   (D) She's a legal secretary

   Answer: (C)

2. Where does Jeanette work?

   （珍德在哪兒工作？）

   (A) At a newspaper

   (B) At an accounting firm

   (C) At a law firm

   (D) At a major corporation

   Answer: (B)

b. Offering a Loan
借錢給朋友

Martina came into Joe's apartment looking very distressed. She put up her hands and was about to expound on the source of her concern, but instead she asked for a drink---a hard drink. Joe was quick to pour her a vodka tonic and let her pour out her problems. Apparently, Martina had fallen behind on rent payment, and she received a notice pinned on her door that the complex would litigate if it didn't receive a payment soon.

Joe was quiet for a while. Then he offered an idea: "Why don't I do you a favor?"

Martina, already catching on to what Joe was indicating, lit up. "Would you really?"

"I'd give you enough to pay for your rent, but you would have to pay me back."

"Oh, I'd be so thankful."

"You'd have to pay me back at five percent interest, though, if you don't pay me back within two months."

"I'd do anything."

中譯

馬蒂娜來到喬的公寓,樣子十分苦惱。她舉起手,一副要訴說她煩惱的來源,然而她卻要求要喝杯酒。喬很快地倒杯伏特加酒給她,並讓她把問題說出。顯然馬蒂娜遲交房租,她收到一張釘在門口的字條。上面說假如沒有很快收到租金,租屋公司就要告她。

喬沈默了一會兒。然後,提出一個主意。「讓我幫個忙好了。」

馬蒂娜了解到喬的意思,輕快了起來。「真的嗎?」

「我會借你錢付房租,但是你要還我。」

「喔。我會很感謝你。」

「假如你沒在兩個月內還我,好要付我百分之五的利息。」

「做什麼我都願意。」

Questions:

1. Why was the complex going to take Martina to court?

（為何租屋公司要與馬蒂娜法庭相見？）

(A) She burnt the apartment complex down

(B) She was squatting

(C) She didn't pay the rent

(D) She broke the contract by moving out without permission

Answer: (C)

2. At what interest was Joe going to charge her?

（喬向她索取多少利息？）

(A) 2%

(B) 3%

(C) 4%

(D) 5%

Answer: (D)

Conversation:

Joe: How about I do you a favor?
（我幫妳，如何？）

Martina: Would you really?
（真的？）

Joe: I could lend you the money...
（我可以借妳錢。）

Martina: Oh, I would be so thankful.
（喔，我會很感謝的。）

Joe: And I'll do so on two conditions...
（我有兩個條件。）

Martina: Anything.
（什麼都可以。）

Joe: You pay me back at 5% interest if you don't pay me back within three months...
（假如你沒在三個月內還我，你要付我百分之五的利息。）

Martina: Okay.
（好。）

Joe: You go on a date with me.
（還有跟我約會。）

Martina: I suppose it couldn't hurt.
（無所謂。）

Questions:

1. How many conditions does Joe ask from Martina?

    （喬向馬蒂娜提出幾個條件？）

    (A) 1

    (B) 2

    (C) 3

    (D) 4

    Answer: (B)

2. What was Joe's second condition?

    （喬的第二個條件是什麼？）

    (A) That Martina lend him money when he needs

    (B) Martina has to clean his car

    (C) Martina has to cook him dinner for two months

    (D) Martina has to go on a date with him

    Answer: (D)

Rodney rushed into Stewart's apartment, out of breath. Stewart was half asleep, hanging himself over a hot bowl of oatmeal. He looked up at the opening of his door and wondered briefly what Rodney wanted.

Stewart thought for a moment. "Aren't you a little late for you work?"

"Yeah, I missed the bus," Rodney replied. "You got any orange juice?"

"Don't you need to get to work?"

"Didn't you just hear me? I missed the bus. Another one's not coming for another hour. So, oh well."

"Well, I'm about to leave. So if you'd like a ride, you can come along with me," Stewart suggested.

"You'd do that?"

"Just for you."

中譯

　　羅尼氣喘吁吁地衝進史都華的公寓。史都華還沒完全睡醒，低著頭在喝一碗熱的燕麥粥。他抬頭望向被打開的門，腦子裡飛快地想著羅尼想幹嘛。

　　史都華想了一下。「你上班不會有點晚了嗎？」

　　「是啊。我錯過巴士了。」羅尼答道。「你有柳橙汁嗎？」

　　「你不用去上班嗎？」

　　「你沒聽到我說的嗎？我錯過巴士了。下一班要一個小時才會來。所以就是這樣。」

　　「我也正要去上班。假如你需要搭車，你可以跟我一起走。」史都華建議。

　　「你願意？」

　　「我就只為你這麼做。」

Questions:

1. What is Rodney late for?

    （羅尼為了什麼事會遲到？）

    (A) Work

    (B) School

    (C) Volunteer work

    (D) Swimming lessons

    Answer: (A)

2. What kind of drink does Rodney want?

    （羅尼想喝什麼？）

    (A) Milk

    (B) Grape juice

    (C) Water

    (D) Orange juice

    Answer: (D)

Conversation:

Stewart: Aren't you a little late for work?
（你上班不會有點晚嗎？）

Rodney: Yeah, I missed the bus.
（是啊，我錯過巴士了。）

Stewart: I could give you a ride, you know?
（我可以讓你搭便車。）

Rodney: Thanks, man.
（多謝了。）

Stewart: I'll be ready in ten minutes.
（我十分鐘就好了。）

Wait down at the picnic tables next to my car.
（在我車子旁的野餐桌等我。）

Rodney: Sure thing, thanks again.
（好，再次謝了。）

Questions:

1. What did Rodney miss?

（羅尼錯過什麼？）

(A) A cab

(B) His girlfriend

(C) The bus

(D) The train

Answer: (C)

2. Where did Stewart tell Rodney to meet him?

（史都華要羅尼在哪裡與他碰面？）

(A) At the door to the apartment complex

(B) At the picnic tables

(C) At the bus station

(D) At the bus stop

Answer: (B)

d. Offering help
幫忙功課

Andi was in the eighth grade. She was struggling a bit in her classes and her parents knew it, too. She was afraid to admit it to them and was too shy to ask for their help. One day, when Andi was busy doing her math homework, her dad was watching her, wondering how much she was struggling.

"Yes Dad?" Andi asked when she noticed her father watching her.

"Nothing. I was just wondering if you wanted any help?" he said gently.

"No, that's okay."

"Are you sure?" he said it casually, through his tone he let it be known that it wouldn't be any bother for him to help her.

"Well, I guess I could use some help."

　　安蒂是八年級學生。她的功課有點困難，她的父母也知道。她害怕向他們坦承，也不敢要求他們幫忙。有一天，安蒂忙著做數學功課，她父親在旁邊看，想著她遇到的困難不知道有多大。

　　「爸，有事嗎？」安蒂問，她注意到父親在看著她。

　　「沒事。我只是在想妳需不需要幫忙？」他溫和地說。

　　「不用，我還可以。」

　　「你確定？」他漫不經心地說，從語調讓她知道，幫忙她，他一點也不會覺得麻煩。

　　「好吧，我想我需要一點協助。」

8

Offering 提供

Questions:

1. What grade was Andi in?

（安蒂幾年級？）

(A) Seventh

(B) Eighth

(C) Ninth

(D) Tenth

Answer: (B)

2. Which class was Andi doing homework for?

（安蒂在做什麼功課？）

(A) Math

(B) English

(C) Science

(D) Music

Answer: (A)

Conversation:

Andi: Yes, Dad?
（有事嗎？爸。）

Dad: Nothing, I was just wondering if you could use any help?
（沒事，我只是在想妳是不是需要協助？）

Andi: Do you know much about Shakespeare?
（你知道多少關於莎士比亞的事？）

Dad: I know a little.
（我知道一點。）

Andi: Well, that's who we're studying in history class right now.
（那是我們現在歷史課正在上的人物。）

Anyway, there's a question about this Marlowe guy and his relation to Shakespeare.
（總之，有個問題在探討這個馬樂威，和莎士比亞的關係。）

Dad: Christopher Marlowe?
（克里斯多福‧馬樂威？）

Andi: Yeah, do you know about him?
（是啊，你知道他嗎？）

Dad: Not really.
（不是很清楚。）

Do you have anything else I could help you with?
（有沒有其他我可以幫妳的？）

Questions:

1. Who was Andi's history class studying?

   （安蒂歷史課正在研讀誰？）

   (A) Robbespiere
   (B) Shakespeare
   (C) Marlowe
   (D) Napoleon

   Answer: (B)

2. Which class was Andi studying for?

   （安蒂正在讀哪一科？）

   (A) Math
   (B) English
   (C) Science
   (D) History

   Answer: (D)

e. Invitation
邀約

Jack's parents were going out of town for the weekend. This didn't happen often, so when it did, Jack figured that it was time to celebrate. He was thinking he'd have a pool party in his backyard, grill up some barbecued pork chops, drink some beer, and have a few friends---guys and girls-over for a good time. Jack picked up the phone and called Steven to tell him what was going on.

"So, you want to come?" Jack asked him.

"Of course, man. Who else should we invite?"

"I guess Janet and Emily. We could tell them to bring some friends."

"How about Roger?" Steven asked.

"He's a good guy too. Tell him to

bring some friends too."

中譯

　　傑克的父母週末要出城。這並不常發生，所以當它發生了，傑克就覺得該是慶祝的時候。他想想可以在後院開泳池派對，烤些豬肉片，喝些啤酒，並邀請一些朋友——男男女女——來段快樂時光。傑克拿起電話打給史蒂芬，告訴他。

　　「你要來嗎？」傑克問。

　　「當然。我們還要邀請誰？」

　　「珍妮跟愛蜜莉。我們可以叫她們帶些朋友來。」

　　「羅傑呢？」史蒂芬問。

　　「他也很好。也叫他帶些朋友。」

Questions:

1. How was Jack inviting people?

    （傑克如何邀請人？）

    (A) Telling them
    (B) Writing them
    (C) Emailing them
    (D) None of the above

    Answer: (A)

2. What is the occasion for the party?

    （派對發生在什麼時候？）

    (A) It's Jack's birthday
    (B) It's Steve's birthday
    (C) Jack's parents are out of town
    (D) It's Jack's bar mitzvah

    Answer: (C)

Conversation:

Steven: Hey Emily, Jack's having this party this weekend.
（嗨！愛蜜莉。傑克這個週末要開派對。）

Emily: Okay.
（好啊。）

Steven: Well, I was wondering if you would like to go with me there.
（我想問妳可以跟我一起去嗎？）

Emily: Yeah, I guess that would be cool. Could I bring some friends?
（好啊，我想那一定很棒。我可以帶朋友去嗎？）

Steven: How many did you have in mind?
（妳想帶多少人？）

Emily: Two of my friends.
（兩個。）

We were all going to get together this weekend and do girl stuff but a party sounds better anyway.
（我們本來這個週末要一起做些女孩家的事，不過派對似乎比較好玩。）

What day is it?
（哪一天？）

Steven: It's on Saturday.
（禮拜六。）

Yeah, bring however many friends you'd like.
The more the merrier.
（帶多少朋友隨妳喜歡。越多越快樂。）

Questions:

1. How many friends is Emily going to bring?

（愛蜜莉要帶多少朋友來？）

(A) One

(B) Two

(C) Three

(D) Four

Answer: (B)

2. What day is the party on?

（派對何時舉行？）

(A) Saturday

(B) Sunday

(C) Friday

(D) Wednesday

Answer: (A)

9. Social Talk

聊天

a. A new neighbor

新鄰居

MP3-40

Victor had recently moved into his new apartment in Dallas, Texas. He had yet to really make any friends and so was always on the lookout. He would watch a person walk to or from one's car, always hoping that that person would come up to him and introduce himself. Once, when an exceptionally attractive woman named Linda walked by, he finally broke the ice and said, "Hello neighbor!"

She turned to him and looked at him as if he had lost his mind. "Hello," she replied back, afraid of being accused of

being impolite. She kept walking.

"My name is Victor. I'm your new neighbor."

Now understanding why he would simply blurt out, "hello neighbor," she stopped and introduced herself as well. "My name's Linda. How long have you lived here?"

中譯

　　維特最近搬進德州達拉斯的新公寓。他尚未交到朋友，所以總是在密切注意。他會看著走向車子的人或從車內出來的人，希望他們會來跟他介紹自己。有一回，一位特別引人注目名叫琳達的女子經過，他終於打破沈默說道：「哈囉！芳鄰！」

　　她轉身，彷彿看著瘋子般地看他。「哈囉。」她回道，以免被誤以為不禮貌。她繼續往前走。

　　「我叫維特。我是妳的新鄰居。」

　　現在瞭解到他會叫出口的原因，她停了下來，並介紹自己。「哈囉，芳鄰。我叫琳達，你在這兒住多久了？」

Questions:

1. To which city did Victor just move?

   （維特搬進了哪個城市？）

   (A) San Antonio, Texas

   (B) Seattle, Washington

   (C) Dallas, Texas

   (D) Tulsa, Oklahoma

   Answer: (C)

2. To or from where were people walking whom Victor watched?

   （維特看著走向何處或走出哪兒的人？）

   (A) An apartment

   (B) A car

   (C) The gym

   (D) Work

   Answer: (B)

Conversation:

Victor: Hello neighbor!
（哈囉，芳鄰！）

Simon: Hey. I haven't seen you around here before.
（嘿，我以前沒在這附近見過你。）

You new here?
（你是新來的嗎？）

Victor: Sure am. Just moved in a week ago.
（當然，我一星期前才搬進來的。）

Simon: Where are you from?
（你從哪兒來的？）

Victor: New York.
（紐約。）

It's quite different down here.
（這兒跟紐約很不一樣。）

Simon: How do you like it?
（你覺得如何？）

Victor: It's not too bad.
（還不錯。）

The only thing I really don't like is the heat.
（我唯一不喜歡的是天氣太熱了。）

Questions:

1. From where did Victor move?

（維特從哪兒搬來？）

(A) Seattle, Washington

(B) Newark, New Jersey

(C) San Francisco, California

(D) New York, New York

Answer: (D)

2. What does Victor not like about Dallas?

（維特不喜歡達拉斯哪一點？）

(A) The heat

(B) The humidity

(C) The people

(D) The mass transit system

Answer: (A)

b. Talking about the election
談論選舉

It's a tendency for most Americans to stray away from politics in conversation, since it's a subject that can cause much division among people. "Never talk about politics or religion," the old adage goes. However, when talk of the war comes up, Joseph always gets riled up and starts talking about the election.

"Who are you going to vote for?" he would ask. His tone would be near accusatory.

"I'm thinking about Nader," Eric, his friend said.

"Don't vote for Nader, he's only going to detract votes away from Kerry. If you don't want Bush to win, you'll have to vote for Kerry."

中譯

　　大部份美國人都會在對話中避免談到政治，因為這是個經常引起人們分裂的議題。俗語說：「千萬別談政治或宗教。」然而，每當談到戰爭，喬斯總是開始激動，並開始談起選舉。

　　他會問，「你要選誰？」。他的聲調近乎控訴。

　　「我想選納達。」他的朋友艾瑞克說。

　　「別選納達，他只會分散凱瑞的票源。你要是不想布希贏的話，就要選凱瑞。」

Questions:

1. "Never talk about politics or _____."

   （千萬別談政治或 _____ ）

   (A) War

   (B) Crime

   (C) Religion

   (D) Race

   Answer: (C)

2. Talking about what gets Joseph all riled up?

   （談到什麼會讓喬斯激動？）

   (A) War

   (B) Drugs

   (C) Rock music

   (D) Education

   Answer: (A)

Conversation:

Joseph: Who are you going to vote for?
（你要選誰？）

Eric: I'm thinking about Nader.
（我要選納達。）

Joseph: Don't vote for Nader.
（別選納達。）

He's only going to detract votes from Kerry and make Bush win.
（他只會分散凱瑞的票源，而讓布希獲勝。）

Do you really think voting for Nader will do anything?
（你真認為選納達會有益處嗎？）

Eric: Look, you asked me who I was going to vote for, so I told you.
（聽著，你問我要選誰，我告訴你了。）

How about this weather?
（你覺得這天氣怎樣？）

Joseph: I can't believe you'd let Bush win.
（我不敢相信你竟要讓布希贏。）

Eric: It sure has been sunny out lately.
（最近都是晴天。）

With a nice breeze too, I like that.
（還有微風，這我喜歡。）

Questions:

1. According to Joseph, what would voting for Nader do?

（據喬斯說，選納達會怎樣？）

(A) Get Nader elected as president
(B) Get Bush elected as president
(C) Get Kerry elected as president
(D) None of the above

Answer: (B)

2. What did Eric try to change the subject to?

（艾瑞克想將話題轉為什麼？）

(A) Class
(B) Girls
(C) Parties
(D) Weather

Answer: (D)

9 Social Talk 聊天

c. News
新聞

Bob sat down at lunch, tired from a long morning at work filled with meetings. Joe sat next to him, pulling out his sandwich and began to eat. He paused and said, "Hey Bob."

"Hey Joe," Bob replied.

"You watch the news, Bob?" Joe asked in between bites.

"I catch it every now and then."

"Did you hear about that cop?"

"What cop?" Bob evidently did not hear about the cop.

"The one who got his foot ran over by someone he was trying to ticket. Terrible thing. The cop should have shot that guy."

"You're kidding?"

"No, really, he should have shot him."

包柏坐下來吃午餐，因早上排滿的會議而感到疲憊不堪。喬坐在他旁邊，拿出三明治開始吃。他停了下來，並說：「嘿，包柏。」

「嘿，喬。」包柏回道。

「你有看新聞嗎？包柏。」喬邊吃邊問。

「我偶而會看看新聞。」

「你知道那個警察嗎？」

「什麼警察？」包柏顯然不知道那個警察。

「那個腳被他開罰單的人輾過的警察。太可怕了。那警察該開槍打那傢伙。」

「你在開玩笑吧？」

「不，我是說真的。他該開槍打他。」

Questions:

1. **What happened on the news?**

（發生什麼新聞？）

(A) Someone's dog ran away

(B) A house caught on fire

(C) A gorilla escaped from the zoo

(D) Someone ran over a cop's foot

Answer: (D)

2. **What would have been Bob's remedy?**

（包柏的補救方法是什麼？）

(A) Cop should have shot him

(B) Cop should have chased him down

(C) Cop should have called for backup

(D) Cop should have ignored him

Answer: (A)

Conversation:

Simon: You watch the news last night?
（你昨晚有看新聞嗎？）

Bob: Nope, didn't catch it.
（沒有，沒看到。）

What happened?
（有什麼事嗎？）

Simon: Some gorilla escaped at the zoo.
（有大猩猩逃出動物園。）

Bob: Oh yeah, I read about that in the newspaper.
（喔，是啊，我在報紙上有讀到。）

Simon: He was chasing down two cops.
（牠追著兩個警員。）

So they shot him to death.
（所以他們把牠射死了。）

Bob: That's too bad.
（太慘了。）

Simon: Yeah, too bad.
（是啊，太慘了。）

They should have had tranquilizers or something to have nailed the poor animal with. Oh well.
（他們應該用鎮定劑或其他東西來捉住那可憐的動物，唉。）

Questions:

1. From where did Bob find out about the gorilla escaping?

（包柏從哪兒知道大猩猩的事？）

   (A) Television news

   (B) Internet news

   (C) Newspaper

   (D) Someone told him about it that morning

   Answer: (C)

2. With what did Simon think the cops should have been armed?

（賽門認為警察應該帶什麼裝備？）

   (A) Stun guns

   (B) Swords

   (C) Nets

   (D) Tranquilizers

   Answer: (D)

d. A new co-worker
新同事

MP3-43

Simon came to work one morning and he noticed that there was someone occupying the office which had been formally empty for three months. "What's this?" he thought to himself. He walked right on past though, acting as if he knew what was going on. He went right over to Fred, his work buddy's office.

"Who's the new girl?" Simon asked. He had noticed that his new co-worker was a female.

"Her name's Angela. She's got a degree in Economics. I haven't met her yet."

"I didn't realize we were hiring," Simon said.

"Neither did I."

中譯

　　一天早上，賽門進了辦公室注意到之前空了三個月的辦公室有人在使用。「怎麼回事？」他心想。但是他卻從那間辦公室前面走過，假裝他很清楚是怎麼一回事。他走到他的工作伙伴瑞得的辦公室。

　　「新來的女孩是誰？」賽門問。他已經注意到他的新同事是個女性。

　　「她叫安琪拉。她擁有經濟學位，我還沒跟她碰面。」

　　「我不曉得我們有徵人。」賽門說。

　　「我也不知道。」

Questions:

1. In what does the new employee have a degree?

（新雇員有什麼學位？）

(A) Business

(B) Mathematics

(C) Economics

(D) History

Answer: (C)

2. How long had the office been empty?

（辦公室空了多久了？）

(A) 1 month

(B) 2 weeks

(C) 6 months

(D) 3 months

Answer: (D)

Conversation:

Simon: So, you're the new employee, huh?
（妳是新來的雇員？）

Angela: As of nine o'clock this morning, I sure am.
（如同現在是早上九點鐘一樣確定，我當然是。）

Simon: What are you going to be doing with us?
（妳將要做什麼工作？）

Angela: I'm going to help you guys close some of your accounts.
（我將幫忙你們總結一些帳目。）

Simon: Oh really? Which ones?
（喔，真的？哪些？）

Angela: Just a few minor ones to start off with.
（只是先從些小帳目做起。）

Like the D'Angelo and the Rodriguez accounts.
（比如 D'Angelo 和 the Rodriguez 的帳目。）

Simon: D'Angelo is one of my accounts.
（D'Angelo 是我處理的帳目之一。）

Angela: I guess we'll be working a lot together.

（我想有很多工作我們要一起處理。）

Simon: Where did you used to work?

（妳之前在哪兒工作？）

Angela: Over at Marius, Inc.

（在馬瑞斯公司。）

They offered me a better pay here.

（這裡的薪水比較高。）

It's a nice office too.

（辦公室也不錯。）

Questions:

1. Which account of Simon's is Angela going to be working on?

   （賽門的哪個帳目是安琪拉要處理的？）

   (A) Rodriguez
   (B) Gilmore
   (C) D'Angelo
   (D) Azure

   Answer: (C)

2. Where did Angela used to work?

   （安琪拉之前在哪兒工作？）

   (A) Gilmore Company
   (B) Marius, Inc.
   (C) April-May Corporation
   (D) Rod Co.

   Answer: (B)

e. A farewell party
歡送會

April had worked for the Manuel Corporation for 13 years when she was offered a better job working for Isaac Stewart, Inc. She had decided that her days at Manuel Corporation had come to an end and to start a new life at her new firm.

Knowing all this, her friends at Manuel Corporation, led by her favorite, Isabelle, decided to throw her a surprise going away party. They had told her there was a meeting planned for 10:30 in the morning, three days before she left, and they had assembled all of her co-workers together to send her off with their best wishes.

When she came into the room and saw all of the balloons, she had instantly understood what they had done for her. "Oh, you guys!" she exclaimed to them, as tears swelled into her eyes. She was going

to miss working with her friends at Manuel Corporation.

中譯

　　雅爾在麥紐爾公司工作了十三年後，以薩克・史都華公司提供她一個更好的職位。她決定結束在麥紐爾公司的工作，並在新公司展開新的生活。

　　得知一切，由伊沙貝拉發起，召集她在麥紐爾公司的朋友，決定為她開個驚喜的離別派對。在她離職前三天，他們告訴她早上十點半有個會議，他們聚集了所有的同事，以最誠摯的祝福為她餞別。

　　當她進到房間，看見滿室的氣球，她立刻明白他們為她所做的事。「喔，你們大家！」她對他們說，眼睛湧出了淚水。她將會想念與朋友們在麥紐爾公司共事的時光。

Questions:

1. How many days before April left was the farewell party?

（離別派對在雅爾離職前幾天舉行？）

(A) 1 day

(B) 2 days

(C) 3 days

(D) 4 days

Answer: (C)

2. Where was April going to work next?

（雅爾接下來要在哪兒工作？）

(A) Manuel Corporation

(B) Isaac Stewart, Inc.

(C) Isabelle Stewart, Inc.

(D) April-May Corporation

Answer: (B)

9 Social Talk 聊天

Conversation:

Isabelle: We should plan a farewell party for April.

（我們該為雅爾舉辦離別派對。）

Donnie: Yeah, I agree. It's going to be so weird without her.

（是啊，我同意。沒有她在，一定很怪。）

Isabelle: We should get her a present too.

（我們也該送她一個禮物。）

Donnie: What did you have in mind?

（妳心裡有何主意？）

Isabelle: Something for her new office, I suppose, so that every time she looks at it she will remember her times here.

（某件適合她新辦公室的東西，這樣她每次見到就會想起在這兒的時光。）

Donnie: How about a nice clock?

（一個漂亮的時鐘，怎麼樣？）

Isabelle: Sounds good to me.

（聽起來不錯。）

Questions:

1. Where would April put the present that Isabelle and Donnie want to buy for her?

（雅爾會把伊沙貝拉跟東尼想買給她的禮物放哪兒？）

(A) At home

(B) In her car

(C) In the office

(D) None of the above

Answer: (C)

2. What are Isabelle and Donnie thinking about buying April?

（伊沙貝拉跟東尼想買給雅爾什麼？）

(A) A clock

(B) A new set of golf clubs

(C) A jacket

(D) A watch

Answer: (A)

9 Social Talk 聊天

10. Modern Life
現代生活

a. Computer
電腦

MP3-45

Amy was an older lady, and she felt somewhat intimidated by younger people working at the same company that she worked for, Grinsfelder, LLP. They could do things on the computer that she couldn't dream of and they could type programs and print things out in colorful displays. She couldn't do anything like that; she has just barely learned how to use the Office Suite. There were always new programs to learn and new ways to program things. She was feeling overwhelmed and she was afraid that her job was at stake.

中譯

　　艾蜜是一位上了年紀的淑女，同樣在葛林佛公司工作，她感受到來自於年輕人的威脅。他們會處理她作夢也想不到的電腦，他們也會輸入程式及彩色列印。她不會做類似的事，她僅能學會如何使用辦公室的軟體。一直有新的程式要學習，以及新的程式處理方法。她感到不知所措並害怕工作面臨危機。

Questions:

1. What program had Amy just learned to use?

（艾蜜學習使用什麼樣的程式？）

(A) The Office Suite

(B) The calendar program

(C) The internet browser

(D) The email system

Answer: (A)

2. Who was Amy intimidated by?

（艾蜜受到來自誰的威脅？）

(A) The boss

(B) The young people at work

(C) Her co-worker Steve

(D) The bartender

Answer: (B)

Conversation:

Amy: I just can't understand how to use this spreadsheet!
（我就是不懂如何使用這個試算表。）

Steve: It's easy. I'll show you.
（很簡單，我弄給你看。）

Amy: What? I don't need anyone to show me!
（什麼？我不需要任何人示範給我看！

Do you think I'm stupid?
（你以為我很笨嗎？）

Steve: No, I don't think you're stupid.
（不，我不認為你笨。）

Amy: You young people think you can march in here and tell us how things are done.
（你們年輕人以為你們可以來到這兒，告訴我們事情該如何做。）

Well, you won't. I've been working here for 37 years.
（但，你不能。我已經在這兒工作三十七年了。）

I know how things are done.
（我知道怎麼做事。）

Steve: Do you want me to show you or not?
（你要不要我示範給你看？）

Questions:

1. What can't Amy figure out how to use?

    （艾蜜不知如何使用什麼？）

    (A) The email
    (B) The operating system
    (C) The word processor
    (D) The spreadsheet

    Answer: (D)

2. What does Amy accuse Steve of thinking she is?

    （艾蜜指控史蒂芬認為她怎樣？）

    (A) Smart
    (B) Ugly
    (C) Stupid
    (D) Pitiful

    Answer: (C)

b. Internet
網際網路

MP3-46

The internet has revolutionized communication technologies. People can access data at speeds never before imaginable. They can research files that once required someone to travel all the way across the country to find in mere seconds. Andrew of Lionheart Industries new this, and when he first saw the revolution coming, he immediately began to update all of his systems so that he would have a real advantage over his competitors. All of the employees had e-mail accounts as soon as the technology became available. He also installed wireless internet access throughout all of his buildings, so that every employee could log in and communicate with any employee anywhere in the country or anywhere in the world.

中譯

　　網路改革了傳播科技。人們可以以從前無法想像的速度取得資料。他們可以在幾秒內搜尋到曾經需要人踏遍全國才能找到的檔案。獅心工業的安德魯知道這點，因此他一見革新降臨，便立刻著手將他的所有系統更新，如此他才能比他的競爭者更具優勢。一旦此項科技可以使用，所有雇員都有電子郵件帳號。他也在整棟建築物裝上無線上網捷徑，如此每位雇員都能上網，並與任何員工在全國各地或世界各地聯繫。

Questions:

1. What kind of access does Andrew have installed in his buildings?

（安德魯在其建築物安裝了什麼？）

(A) T1

(B) wireless

(C) Cable

(D) DSL

Answer: (B)

2. What did all of the employees get as soon as the technology became available?

（一旦科技可行，每位雇員都有什麼？）

(A) Internet
(B) Computers
(C) E-mail accounts
- (D) Cars

Answer: (C)

Conversation:

Victor: How did you foresee the Internet being so useful to the company?
（你如何預見網路對公司有極大幫助？）

Andrew: Anyone could have seen it.
（任何人都可以預見。）

That kind of communicative ability.
（那種傳播能力。）

It would boost the competitive edge to any corporation.

（它能提升任何一家公司的競爭優勢。）

Victor: What is the most important system that you have set up on the internet?

（你在網路上設立了何種最重要的系統？）

Andrew: I would say the system that our sales division has set up.

（我認為是建立了銷售分區的系統。）

It allows a communication between every division in our company to know exactly what needs to be shipped and when it needs to be shipped as soon as the order is made.

（它讓我們公司的每個部門一旦在接獲訂單時，能夠準確知道何者需要運輸以及何時需要運送。）

No mistakes are made because it's automated.

（不會有錯誤，因為它是自動化的。）

Questions:

1. What does the internet boost for any corporation?

   （網路會為任何一家公司提升什麼？）

   (A) Cash flow

   (B) Investment opportunities

   (C) Worker confidence

   (D) Competitive edge

   Answer: (D)

2. Which division of Lionheart Industries uses the internet most efficiently?

   （獅心工業運用網路最有效的是哪個部門？）

   (A) Production

   (B) Sales

   (C) Management

   (D) Operations

   Answer: (B)

讀霸！多益閱讀模擬測驗

英語系列：50

作者／張瑪麗 Steve King
出版者／哈福企業有限公司
地址／新北市板橋區五權街16號
電話／(02) 2808-6545　傳真／(02) 2808-6545
郵政劃撥／31598840　戶名／哈福企業有限公司
出版日期／2018年9月
定價／NT$ 329元 (附MP3)

全球華文國際市場總代理／采舍國際有限公司
地址／新北市中和區中山路2段366巷10號3樓
電話／(02) 8245-8786　傳真／(02) 8245-8718
網址／www.silkbook.com　新絲路華文網

香港澳門總經銷／和平圖書有限公司
地址／香港柴灣嘉業街12號百樂門大廈17樓
電話／(852) 2804-6687　傳真／(852) 2804-6409
定價／港幣110元 (附MP3)

email／haanet68@Gmail.com
網址／Haa-net.com
facebook／Haa-net 哈福網路商城

國家圖書館出版品預行編目資料

讀霸!多益閱讀模擬測驗 / 張瑪麗, Steve
King合著. -- 新北市：哈福企業, 2018.09
　　面；　公分. -- (英語系列；50)

ISBN 978-986-96282-2-8(平裝附光碟片)

1.多益測驗

805.1895　　　　　　　　　107009967

哈福

哈福